To Laurie —
... end in letters

D1279327

SCAPEGOATS:
The Goat Protocols

Andrew Grell

GOLDEN FLEECE PRESS

Golden Fleece Press
PO Box 1464,
Centreville, VA 20122
www.goldenfleecepress.com

Special discounts are available on quantity purchases by corporations, associations, and others. For details, contact the publisher at the address above.

Epub ISBN 13:   978-1-942195-59-7
Mobi ISBN 13:   978-1-942195-62-7
Print ISBN 13:   978-1-942195-61-0
Pdf   ISBN 13:   978-1-942195-60-3

Printed in the United States of America

First Edition

10 9 8 7 6 5 4 3 2 1

IN MEMORIAM

Our intrepid huntress, Blue Nora Mae Breyer-Grell, 2009 – 2018

She would climb any height; track, stalk, flush, or find any creature, quiet or quick; judge any dispute; heal any ache or pain; and love eternally.

TO MELODY

Leviticus 16:21-22
> And Aaron shall lay both his hands upon the
> head of the live goat, and confess over him
> all the iniquities of the children of Israel,
> and all their transgressions in all their sins,
> putting them upon the head of the goat,
> and shall send him away by the hand of a
> fit man into the wilderness:
> And the goat shall bear upon him all their
> iniquities unto a land not inhabited: and he
> shall let go the goat in the wilderness.

PROLOGUE: KOEN THE GOAT
WHAT IS NOW THE NETHERLANDS, DAWN OF SETTLED AGRICULTURE.

The goat wasn't pulling a cart, but he felt more weighed down than he'd felt from any load he had pulled. There was no answer to his "Mother, Mother, I am lost" bleating. The sand didn't look like it would provide anything green. He thought freedom from the camp might be interesting, no head-butting, nobody stealing his hair. But yells and hoots and even some rocks met him when he tried to turn back home, and he thought he heard the "Help Me!" bleat from his brother. *Let me just be a camp goat again, I won't complain.* He didn't know why he was cast out, but the only thing to do was to keep moving.

For three days the goat walked, each step heavier than the next, and each more infuriating because he still couldn't figure out what load he was carrying. On the fourth day, he saw a circle of rocks, and from the circle water was coming out in a stream. Well, as long as he could drink, he couldn't give up. Goats don't give up, it's the Code of the Goats, walk or climb, search or protect, but keep being a goat.

For another three days, he followed the stream. On the seventh day of exile, he saw a tamarisk tree in the distance. He let out his excitement bleat, even though there was no goat to hear. Food! Green leaves to eat, and the sweet-sweet on those leaves, too!

Sated, he kept on following the stream. And on the final day of his ignorance, he saw another goat! Family! The goat had a sledge tied to it, but it wasn't pulling, and a man was beating the goat. *Have these people never heard of carts?*

And then his eyes were opened.

CAP the GOAT, and NAN
WEED, CALIFORNIA, THE PRESENT

There are truck stops and there are truck stops, and Pilot is for drivers who know the difference between truck stops and TRUCK STOPS. Showers bright, shiny, squeaky clean; hooks and cubbies ergonomically maximized. Three hundred flavors, styles, and sizes of jerky, and that doesn't include the pemmican. And what a spot! Weed is smack in the middle of five—count 'em—five National Forests. If green had its own rainbow, the view from Weed would be every color. And then in the fall... every color in anybody's rainbow, from IR to UV2.

Nan, a lean, clean, never-mean long-hauler, parked her Pete in the plaza, patted the dashboard plastic Saint-with-no-name on the head, climbed down from the cab and scanned for anyone she might know— friend or foe both. Everyone liked her naturally-curly hair, just like Charlie Brown's little sister, Sally, and the vestiges of laughing freckles. Sadly, some people liked them a little too much. Nan had no idea that what was coming was outside of the normal set of friends and foes.

"*Hey babe, are you headed north?*"

"Who said that?" asked Nan. The voice sounded like Mr. Antonier, her AP Calc teacher, but she remembered he had passed on two years ago.

"*Me, look down, I'm right here.*"

"AHH! OHMYGOSH OHMYGOSH OHMYGOSH you're a goat!"

"*That's right, and you're a truck driver. We all have our jobs to do. My job is to be a goat, and hopefully, your job is to give me a ride to Kalispell,*" Stated the piebald little goat.

2

"You're a goat, goats don't talk, am I losing it?" asked Nan, both to herself and the goat. Long haulers had a penchant for practical jokes.

*"Maybe. I mean, you **are** asking a goat if you're losing it. But don't worry, you're not losing it. And I'm not really talking; I'm putting words inside your head. I can do that, but unfortunately, although I can steer and use an automatic, I can't work the pedals or use a double-clutch. And my license expired."*

"License? Expired? What?"

"Take it easy, just kidding you. Kidding, get it? Look, it's a long ride to the high plains, you can use a good running gag," the goat said.

"I must be losing my mind...talking to a—what, a goat-hiker?"

"I'll tell you what. Go around and take a look at the landing gear. You're going to see a twenty-dollar bill stuck to the driver's side one. Held on with goat spit, by the way. That is, if you aren't losing your mind and I am a goat. Unless you're really and truly bonkers and you put it there yourself. You're not sleep-driving, are you? No Ambien to get you to bed, bennies to get you up? They don't make bennies any more, do they? And where would you have gotten goat spit and goat hairs in the spit without a goat, huh?"

"And how did you know I was going to Kalispell?"

"Well, a bunch of boxes of tchotchkes labeled Greetings from Glacier National Park was kind of a hint. Plus the T-Shirts and that penny candy. Is there a gift shop anywhere in the world that doesn't sell colored sticks of solidified sucrose? Does it still cost a penny anywhere? It was either you or the Coca Cola truck, and I hate the sound of sloshing. Chop Chop, walk around, get the twenty, confirm that you're not hallucinating, help me up into the sleeper, and I'll tell you what to do with the money."

"I'm not...ummm... I'm not licensed to transport live animals..."

"That's fine, get me a tie and an American flag pin and I can pass for Senator Larry Craig."

"Larry Craig?"

"Are you sure you're a truck stop regular? Never mind. I'm Cap, by the way. With whom may I say I have the pleasure?"

"Nan. Nancy Unger, folks call me Nan. How come you don't know that if you're in my head?"

"I'm not in your head, I'm just putting words there. It only goes one way. If you want me to know something I don't already know, you'll have to just tell me."

"Well, let's see what it is you did to my landing gear. Hmmm... Well, okay, there it is. Nice trick. Looks like the steering wheel is still connected to the tires and I'm not dreaming."

Nan, by nature adventurous, decided to play along. She tossed her laundry bag into the sleeper and made sure the bud in the vase—an actual original Volkswagen Beetle bud vase—was straight. And then for good measure decided to tuck the "If this truck's rockin'" sticker under the seat.

"Okay, hop up… Can you hop up?"

"We can climb trees, I should be able to climb into a truck. As you keep going north on I5, when we get out of California, we'll make a stop in Medford, where there's going to be an off-track betting establishment."

ᑕᕼᕮᐯY, BᕮᖇT, and ᖴᖇIᕮᑎᗪS
UPPER PENINSULA, MICHIGAN,
AN ISOLATED SPOT. THE PRESENT

Geography in the UP is, shall we say, creative. Following the St. Mary's River (which is about as much a river as the East River in New York City is) back east from Sault Ste. Marie, we take some bends and encounter two Island Number Ones and one Island Number Three but seem to be short an Island Number Two. We pass the Chippewa area (yup, we're in Gitchie Goomie territory now) and come to the superlatively verdant Methodist Reserve. This a great spot for Engineer Goats to go about their nerdy business without being interrupted: north of where the farms start and not in any hunting areas either. And hopefully no one would notice a dropped slide rule in the undergrowth or what looks like a torsion pendulum depending from a crook in a twisty tree. Only the cognizant would recognize the marker for the camp entrance: a pocket protector stuck with sap onto the bark of a tree.

"Halt! Who goes there? Friend or phony? No one may pass into the camp of the Ungulate Engineers without submitting to the Question," asked Bert, the Head Nerd—sorry, Chief Engineer.

"C'mon, Bert, it's me, Chevy. We're year-neighbors, and I was BEFORE you."

"The Question!"

"Question! He must answer the Question!" came the chorus of the Bert's friends.

"The Question! All who seek to pass must answer!"

Chevy decided to humor his friends; after all, what else have they got? *"Geez, okay, okay, is that what you've come up with because you can't get those propeller beanies over your horns? What, oh Ungulate Engineers, is the Question that I may answer if I would pass?"*

"*What do you get when you cross a goat and a watermelon?*" asked a big Sable Saneen nanny. Odd for a city goat to be out here.

"Bl*@t. Bl*@t. Bl*@ty bl*@t bl*@t," Chevy complained. "*Leibnitz was still learning to count when that came out. Watermelon, Goat, cosine theta.*" "Bl*@t."

"*Pass, Chevy Goat, friend of Engineers!*"

SOPHIA
SOMEWHERE WE'RE NOT SURE OF. RIGHT NOW

You can call me Sophia; if you can't pronounce Chanukkah, you'll never be able to pronounce my real name. I've been around a long time. I know a lot of stuff—most of it just stuff, but some of it critical. Some of that is stuff that *you* couldn't possibly know. And I have friends in *very* high places. You can trust me.

Here's something I know: Why are a goat with gambling issues and a not-so-secret consortium of goat engineers heading to Kalispell, Montana? That's an easy one. It's the only place in North America with an international airport where goats on the road, or visible from the road, isn't remarkable at all.

If these goats and the rest of those coming to the Great Continental Assembly don't keep their appointment, the world will keep spinning, but that spin might start getting nutated and precessed into a not very comfortable wobble. Figuratively speaking, of course.

Maybe.

BO THE GOAT, and JIMMY
MASSAPEQUA PARK, LONG ISLAND, NEW YORK. THE PRESENT

Sandy had hit Massapequa hard, especially in the Canal Zone. New York Risable (as the rebuilding program was less than affectionately known) had finally paid to have Jimmy's house elevated 12 feet. Jimmy, an Iowa farm boy type, oddly out of place in the New York Metro area, took advantage of the situation to rig a "tree house" behind the breastwork of his parents' newly raised home. It was an ideal situation to keep his new friend, Bo, a billy goat with tragicomic floppy ears, off his parents' radar. Bo smoothly extricated himself from the hanging chair—all the furniture in the treehouse was hanging—and got right to the point. His own point, anyway; Jimmy was still getting used to a talking goat.

"So let me get this straight. You've got a neural net going , inductive recursion, have I got that right? That means it keeps learning? Heuristic? That means it can take shortcuts? And you've ganged the screen-saver idle time from everyone in your class? And you're using it to do what, have it autoplay Kreplachians versus T'sharvs? And it plays so well you win weapons and armor which you sell on EBay to ordinary players? Do I have that right? Smart. Very smart. Could you be smarter?"

"I'm having a meaningful conversation with a goat. How much smarter than that can somebody be?" Jimmy said.

"Listen Jimmy... "

"No, you listen, Bo. First of all, it's *Klatchians versus P'tavs*, not whatever you said. Details matter, haven't you said that?"

"Let me put this another way, Jim. Do you think your neural net could be put to better use?"

"Like what? You mean like helping somebody? To do what, exactly?"

"Well, you've already done that, haven't you? Helped Karen by using your net to program her battle robot? Got her on TV. Got her a scholarship. Can you think of anything else your net can program?"

"My specialty is shooting things and blowing stuff up. Karen did all of the design on the 'bot, I just got the algorithms straightened out. Do we really need more stuff blown up and shot?"

"Oy. For a smart kid... Your skull is as thick as my cousin's, and he's a Mountain Goat Ram. Think outside of yourself."

"Somebody already invented self-driving cars. Those are real pro algorithms, but the project still isn't soup yet."

"Now you're getting close. Think of anyone else who might could use an automated sensor and algorithm system to get around?" asked the ungulate, sensing Jimmy was about to get it. Bo didn't know which was a tougher chew, getting young James to work on difficult code, or getting him some empathy.

"Like blind people? Don't they have dogs or something? And hey, you can talk, how come there aren't any seeing-eye goats, huh?"

"You know it's only some of us. You tested it out yourself. Only certain people can hear us. Half of your class must have passed by me at the parking lot fence, you were the only one who heard me. We're stuck with each other. I have a job to do, getting you to do something good with your net. You have a job to do, calling Karen, having her design a robot seeing-eye dog, then having your net program it. A girl in Sacramento put out a robot cane that can warn of obstacles; she won the national science fair. Think of how much more can be done with GPS directions, facial recognition, traffic avoidance routines. We all have our jobs to do. By the way, the wire-head thing isn't really attractive to girls. I'm not saying you're gonna get schtupped from this, but a humanitarian outlook and public recognition couldn't hurt."

"Schtupped?"

"Look it up."

9

NAN and CAP
MEDFORD, OREGON

The ride north on Interstate 5 to Medford takes you through the Rogue Valley, one of the best places in Oregon to get a sun tan, if you only want to tan for about four hours a day. The Siskiyous to the east and the bottom of the Cascades to the west keep the rain out—a welcome respite from the perpetually damp Pacific Northwest. At the top of the valley is Medford, a thriving little city with a recently-revived downtown area, and in Medford is the place sports fans would think of when they think of Heaven, the Lava Lanes bowling, partying, gaming, and drinking complex. The sports bar has more TV screens than the old Soccer Fan Fantasy commercial. Some of those screens show live horse racing, and Lava Lanes has an Off-Track Betting franchise to take the action.

Nan and Cap rode into town, Cap managing to clamber down from the sleeper, and finally telling Nan what the $20 was for.

"Now, handicapping is not just a numbers game. If you want to handicap with numbers, fine, just put the track odds into a spreadsheet, then, and ya gotta type really fast for this next bit, key in the odds on the tote board at one minute before post time, hit the button, and see which horse had the biggest percent change," Cap explained. *"Smart money bets last, and now you've figured out the smart money pick. Then haul ass to the hundred-dollar window and shout your bet. You can get plenty of good wins that way, but there's one problem. If you try to make an industrial scale bet, you'll weight the pool until your payoff drops the final win price to below your advantage of knowing the smart pick. It's just a good party trick, really, okay for pizza and beer money but you can't get rich that way. No, if you want to handicap, you have to handicap the trainer's head, that's where the action is."*

"Why are you telling me this? I'm not much of a gambler and I don't really know much about horses except that they like carrots and apples and that a Western saddle is bigger than an English saddle. Oh, and apparently they get better shampoo than we do."

The horse connection is incidental; I'm trying to give you some valuable information, it's the least I can do for getting you to give me a lift. But now pay attention. Go down to the sports bar, find the horse race betting kiosk, and put the $20 on Lord Darned Socks in the seventh race at Santa Anita.

"A situation like this doesn't come around very often. The seventh is a stakes race, all the weights are identical, no allowances given for anything, not even the apprentice allowance. Socks is a shipper from Florida, being ridden by Jill Quincy, a single-bug apprentice who has been burning up the track at Gulfstream Park. Question: Why would the trainer want, and the owner pay for, shipping the horse cross country, along with Jill, only to lose her five-pound allowance?"

"Because they know something about Jill's relationship to Socks, and...let me see...they know something about Socks' relationship to... The West Coast? Oranges? Hollywood producers? No... They know something about him and another horse. They know he's going to win, and why. You handicapped the trainers head."

"When you can snatch the tin can from my mouth, grasshopper, it will be time for you leave... Morning line odds for Socks are 70 to 1."

"Do you actually eat tin cans?" Nan narrowed her eyes.

"Well, not me personally. I'm a hay and ivy kind of goat. But some of us are not very bright, I must admit, especially, apparently, Bill Grogan's goat. Don't ask, it's a song."

CHEVY, BERT, aNd OThERS.
THE METHODIST RESERVE NERD CAMP

"Hail, Goat Engineers! I, Chevy the Goat, having answered the riddle correctly and having passed into this illustrious collegium, beseech you to impart information."

"Hi, Chev! Been a while. Where's your friend Koziolek? And what can we do for you?" Bert asked, rubbing a haunch against a handy tree. Bert, an Alpine, couldn't wait to get to the high plains and higher mountains.

"You didn't make the last assembly, so I guess you haven't heard. Koz wound up getting some Polish kid working for the U.N. to put together a modular, scalable, each one teach one education bootstrap system. Perfect for high mountains and deep jungles and inner cities alike.

"The Pontifex of the Augustus of the West accepted it to clear the St. Brice's Day slaughter. That was pretty magnanimous of him; The new PontAugWest is a Roman Catholic, Irish. So Koz made it to a petting zoo, I heard it was in Trieste. Chaffhaye and ivy and the occasional apricot and handful of Chex, and a bath twice a week.

"And some of us chipped in and got him shoes; I'm guessing he'll be the only capra not barefoot. Not that shoes will do anything for him now... Anyway, he was always good with kids. Get it? Kids? That never gets old. So, you and your brainy flock down here, what do you know about the stratosphere up there?"

"I know it's really cold and windy as well as being utterly devoid of alfalfa. Not a fit place for a goat, I can tell you that. What did you have in mind?"

"And what about this Carnot fellow and his cycle?"

"Junior High stuff. It's in the same textbook that has the picture of Einstein holding an anvil in an elevator. Reservoir of hot on one side, Reservoir of cold on the other, wall in between them. Punch a hole in the wall, put in a turbine, the hot

rushes into the cold side, the turbine spins, and you've got an engine. Of course, a plain goat cart was good enough for Porgy."

"Bert, how would you and your bleating flock like to fly a kite to the petting zoo?"

SOPhIA
NOW

Anyone like Gouda cheese? Let me take you on a little trip to the Low Countries, Holland, a few thousand years before delft, wooden shoes, dykes, and windmills. I'm sure some people hearing my story are from Brooklyn, and may have actually attended New Utrecht High School. This is a story of the original Breukelen in the old Utrecht. The folks there had just recently developed the ability for adults to drink milk and not get sick.

The children started growing up bigger and stronger, and the folks had more time to work on figuring stuff out—but also for getting into trouble, especially since wine had also recently been introduced. One day Aart, not really known for thinking things through, reasoned (if that term can be reasonably applied to Aart) that all of the goats looked pretty much alike, and if he enticed someone else's goat with apples to follow him to his own field, no one would be the wiser.

When Coos came to his field for shearing, he realized there was a goat missing—Wotan, one of his favorites. Coos began walking around the village, not really thinking he could tell Wotan from other goats at a distance, but hoping the goat or a sign of him would turn up. And he began calling, "Wotan, Wotan!" and sure enough when he passed Aart's field, Wotan came running. Goats, of course, know their own names and are hard-wired to respond to calls.

Fine. A goat was lost, a goat was found. But Coos thought Aart should pay a penalty for his theft; Aart, of course, did not agree. After Coos smacked him in retribution, Aart hit his head on a boulder in the field and died. Manslaughter in the Low Country. And this tragedy was on top of a year of bad behavior, with people drinking this new wine stuff and winding up with each other's spouses, causing no end of fights. So Arduinna, who was what passed for a moral compass in the village, called everyone to the Sacred Oak Grove. Every family to brought one goat. She chose by lot two goats, Koen, and Dyveke. Everyone in the village took turns putting their hands on the Koen goat, to give it all of their bad deeds, and then they shooed it out of the grove, farther away from town. Dyveke was dinner.

The following month, a family from the village went to attend the wedding of their kin in the next village over. When they arrived, they were warmly greeted by their cousin Friya and her family.

"Did your village happen to lose a goat?" Friya asked. Oldrik kissed his cousin but then paused, considering the awkwardness of the situation. How would their neighbors react if they thought they were deliberately sent a goat laden with bad deeds? Oldrik figured it would be better not to add another bad deed to the list, so he told his cousin the story. Then Friya related their village's half of the tale.

"That goat was spooky from the moment it showed up on the green last month. It went around looking at people, as if he were judging them. Sometimes, he would climb a tree and look down on people. Or maybe he just liked the leaves from higher up. We can't know, but it was strange.

"Then one day he saw Rijkert in his field beating his son Tijn. I'll admit, I would stop and watch that goat when I saw him do anything strange. And this was certainly strange. I saw Rijkert and Tijn talking— talking!—to the goat. I didn't hear the goat say anything, he would just move his head up and down or side to side, like he was paying attention, but who can tell? Goats do that anyway. Tijn is not very bright, and I guess that Tijn couldn't tell what was a weed and what was a crop, so Rijkert was trying to beat it into him. Then Rijkert left to go back to his hut.

"The goat led Tijn through the field. Sometimes he would stop and pull a plant out of the ground with his teeth. It was always a weed. Then, they would resume their walk, the goat passing by the crop plants and stopping at another weed. Tijn pulled it out, and the goat licked his face. They both seemed to enjoy that. Finally, Rijkert came back with a basket of dried fruits from the last harvest. When Tijn pulled out a weed, Rijkert would give him a sweet. After three more sweets, Rijkert and the goat left the field to sit in the shade, and Odin strike me down right here if Tijn didn't get every weed and not one stalk of barley.

"The next day, Rijkert went to our wise woman—you remember Drika, don't you? She blessed your little boy the last time you were here. He had her assemble all of the village on the green, and then gave his speech:

"'If you are in authority over someone, do not punish him for not doing what he does not know how to do. Do not ask someone to do something unless you are certain he knows how to do what you ask. In this way, people can learn without fear, people can do the things they know to do, and every thing will get done by someone who knows how to do it. In this way there will be more things being done and our village will increase in provender and happiness.'

"And then Drika said, 'You have chosen me as your wise woman, and I say, the words of Rijkert are wise. From now on, let this be our way.'

"Then the goat walked over to the spot where Rijkert and Drika had stood, and peed on it, and then left to find some ivy and to see if there were any dried fruits left in Rijkert's bag."

NAN and CAP
MEDFORD, OREGON

"So what do I do with this money? Do I get to keep it?" Nan was holding about two weeks' pay in cash in her hands.

"Nan, if what you wanted was money, you probably wouldn't have heard me when I talked to you. You might have had a part of yourself put the $20 on the landing gear, but is there any part of your head that could have handicapped Socks to win? What's better, having $1,378 dollars in your pocket, or having the sure and certain knowledge that there's something going on? Something like, let's say, **talking goats?"**

"Strictly speaking, I have both the money and the knowledge. And as far as I can see, there's *only one* talking goat. But okay, you've been level with me all the way. What's supposed to happen with the money?"

"When you were in the bar, did you notice a woman sitting alone, probably had a notebook, possibly a slide rule. Do you know what that is? She may have been muttering to herself and thumbing through a chemistry textbook."

"First of all, Mister, um, Smarty Pantsless, I do know what a slide rule is and I can use one. My training driver was, like, 79 or something. He said smart drivers always had a slide rule in the glove box to figure out fuel use, times, compare routes, all that stuff. He said a calculator wasn't as good. A slide rule doesn't need batteries and you can't key a wrong number into it. And it forces you to know what you're doing before you use it. And yes, I think there was a head case at the bar, but that isn't really unusual for a bar. What about her?

"Go back down and strike up a conversation with her. Tell her the slide rule story, ask her where she got her shoes, anything. She's about ready to pop, with any luck she'll tell you about her project. She's working on an enzyme that can reduce

any carbohydrate—starch, sugar, cellulose—and there's an awful lot of wood pulp cellulose in Oregon—to methane. Not to mention the fact that methane doesn't generate particulates, and when waste carbohydrates lay around, they just wind up putting carbon into the air.

"But she needs proof of concept before she can talk to the venture capitalists. She's an independent researcher. She doesn't have university support and she can't get a grant, especially since the wood chip project comes up every time there's an energy crisis and never goes anywhere. If she cannibalizes everything in her basement lab and maxes out her credit card, she's probably only one or two thousand dollars away from dumping wood chips and switch grass into a tank and having it fart.

"Offer her the money. Rip a page out of her notebook, write up a contract with 5% going to Angels Among Us pet recue and 5% to libraries to pay for online scientific research database subscriptions. Have the bartender sign and witness it. That's all, then it's on to Kalispell."

"So, what's in Kalispell, anyway? Got a hot date? Collecting a stud fee to feed your gambling addiction? Blue week timeshare? Seeing how well those hooves do on a glacier? That's why I requested this route, by the way. My folks took me here when I was a little girl, walking on the glacier was the most fun I ever had."

"Actually, it's a date with about a hundred Nannies and Billies, plus any of their facilitators—that's you, by the way—and twelve extremely connected people. It's a blast. And I'm sure you'll get a chance to watch me slide on the ice."

sophia

The idea of a goat to take away the bad actions of camps, towns, and villages started propagating, but slowly. One goat would show up at a virgin community and do its job. Maybe the people would get the idea, maybe they wouldn't. Maybe they would send out their own goat the following year, maybe they wouldn't. The maximum participation increase was limited to one new goat for each participating settlement. Eventually, the practice reached the top of the Balkan Peninsula, to what would eventually become Hungary, where Etvash Goat had some thoughts along these lines.

Etvash had finished his mission to the cluster of huts along the Danube, but rather than resume a life concerned only with finding the greenest leaves, he set off on a mission to a new town. He kept going after that, and after that, until he thought he had actually done some good. If this habit propagated back to the Lowlands and the Sacred Oak Groves, each iteration would be one, plus two—the number of participating places the second year, plus the third year's goats. If there were about 500 places sending out this year, in seven years there would be triple the number of participating towns as there would have been under the old system. That was a maximum, of course, and didn't account for goat loss, but things could really start to happen. If only there were a quicker way to get the message out, and give it some authority. Which brings us to the goat born as Enoch.

THE WILDERNESS OF SIN
1200 BCE

Imagine sand and rocks, rocks and sand, the occasional out-of-place shrub trying to earn a living. Now imagine a camp of three million people wandering around. Or maybe only 300 people. Either way. That was Sinai at the Bronze Age / Iron age border.

"Phineas! Phineas!"

"What? Who? What? Who is that?"

"Phineas, Phineas. Around here I thought that when you hear a voice calling your name and you didn't see anyone, the correct response was 'Here I am.'"

"Okay, okay, so here I am, who are you and where are you? What do you want?"

"I'm right here, in the pen you use to hold the animals waiting to be sacrificed. I'm the one not tied up. I'll stomp my feet one time for each of the wives of Jacob. Come get me and take me out of the pen. Stomp. Stomp. Stomp. Stomp."

"A goat? Goats can't talk. I'm the High Priest. Whoever's doing this better stop right now. I'm sure whoever you are can remember what happened the last time someone ticked me off."

"Oh, I remember that. Who could forget? That was quite an act of marksmanship. But what about you, Phineas, don't you remember what happened the week before that? Did you or did you not see Balaam talking to a donkey? Don't you think goats are maybe at least a bit smarter than donkeys?"

"Fair point. That donkey was being blocked by an angel. How do I know you're not being blocked by a demon?"

"Demon, really? You've heard God and you've seen angels. Have you ever seen a demon? As you say, you're the High Priest. Do you really think there are creatures wandering around who can do what angels can, but without the sanction

of God? Listen to what I have to say. Then decide if it is demonic or not. If it is not demonic, do what I tell you."

"What is your name, goat, so when I am asked who told me to do whatever it is you want me to do, I can tell them."

"I-AM-WHAT-I-EAT is my name. But I don't think you're going to need to use it. I'm happy to let you take credit for this. I understand your Grandpa and your great uncle are writing some books. One of the books has a pretty long list of killing animals for sacrifices. How about, somewhere in the middle of the list, let's say, maybe just before the incense, you let one of the animals live and do something useful?"

SOPHIA

The "scapegoat" was in current use for over a thousand years in Syria before it made its way—via the brave-hearted goat now called I-AM-WHAT-I-EAT—into a text that would actually survive the ages and not have to be dug up out of the sand. Of course, nobody knew what was happening to that bad stuff being carried off, or who was in charge of the hazardous waste processing. Somewhere between Etvash and I-AM—who was willing to risk talking with a guy with a lot of very sharp knives and was also quite skilled at the javelin—the concept of the Idea Goat was born. You've already met some of them, Bert and the Ungulate Engineers. But the best Idea Goat of them all had to be Goat-EL, the first of the Research Goats, a Haggis goat from Scotland, with her left legs slightly shorter than than right. So she can run around the mountains. Widdershins, of course. Here is an excerpt of her presentation from the 400th Continental Great Assembly, just outside of Davos, Switzerland:

Fellow goats, revered Priests, honored guests, fellow goat travelers without whom this conference would not be possible, I am humbled to address this august assemblage. As unused to public speaking as I am, I was advised to 'open with a joke.' Although I finally found a goat joke, all I can remember is the punch line, so here goes: 'Of course he has the manners of a pig, he's a Boer goat.' I hope I have you sufficiently warmed up by that to put me at my ease for the rest of my presentation.

I cannot say that we are fighting a losing battle, despite the dismal numbers. Here we are, in an age of marvels, operating under the auspices of an enlightened organization, and we've only cleared up to the Stockholm Bloodbath. I cannot say we are losing because it is our consistent observation that people prefer to do good; all it takes is to open their eyes to good. What I present to you today is a mathematical method of clearing the most bad per unit goat.

Since the days of the Compact with Phineas, we have had a more or less formal codification of what it means to do good. Put a fence around your roof so playing children don't fall off and kill themselves. Don't spread gossip around. Feed the hungry. Clothe the naked. Raise up those who are bowed down. Tend to the sick. But more importantly follow the way to make sure there is enough food, that people don't become sick, that people can stand up by themselves. These protocols share a single common element, that people must understand and take into account the situations of other people, and goats and other animals for that matter.

I am a logician and a mathematician, not a philosopher, so I can't accurately use the word "empathy" in a rigorous or technical sense. Never the less, I will use that term as a metric in the equation I am now going to derive and present.

Although watching a goat write equations on a board with chalk in her teeth is always good for a laugh, we can skip the math and come straight to the point.

And so we can now see that

$$\sum_{i=1}^{i=n} \log(e) = \sum_{i=1}^{i=n} h + f(k)$$

Or, in plain bleat, the sum of the logarithm of empathy of the individual members of a society predicts the sum of happiness in that society. The trailing correction factor will make this an equality, and will be determined by observation of what happens on the field — should we adopt a strategy based on this equation.

For the less mathematically inclined of the attendees, the logarithm term means that small increases in empathy for a large number of people accomplish much more than even very large increases in a small number of people. And if my peers reviewing this presentation accept my calculations, we will have a formal strategy: get the greatest number of people involved for each operation we undertake. This is a rigorous determination of the fastest possible method of clearing the bad.

She received the loudest bleating and thundering of hooves since Betsy Goat showed John Jay that "peace" should be at the top of the list when negotiating peace treaties.

soph1a
BROWSING DOWN THE TAMARISK PATH
OF COMPROMISE, 2ND CENTURY CE

I hope you've been enjoying the goat antics and weren't disheartened by the math. Knowledge and Wisdom are complementary attributes, it's true. Neither really works well without the other, but sometimes they can be the oil and water type of complements. While each person's wisdom may be different from any other person's wisdom, the trouble starts when people think their knowledge is different from other peoples'.

Fortunately for you, it's conflict, antagonism, and trouble that make a story. I-AM's compact with Phineas lasted for hundreds of years— through years of people still worshipping trees and years of reformation; whether there was one kingdom or two; whether or not people went down to Gaza on a Saturday night (somehow Dagon's temple prostitutes were a bigger draw than watching animals get their throats slit), before or after the exile; before, during, or after Alexander and then the Seleucids; during Roman occupation—there was only one High Priest who could authorize the acceptance of sacrifices. Well, once there was a home team and an away team, but they never fulfilled their duties concurrently. One attempt was made by Eli to have his sons serve as Deputy Co-High Priests, but that didn't work out very well for them.

From the very beginning of this story, the people of each place had their own traditions and kept them, usually respecting the traditions of other places, sometimes laughing at them when they got home. Yet still, everyone had a more or less clear understanding of things that were good and things that were bad, and those understandings typically overlapped from place to place.

Then, as is their wont, people started putting too much thought into something that should have remained simple. This only increased when beliefs, stories, and traditions started getting written down. "Here it is in black tar oil" or "Here it is carved into a rock" or a stele, or an obelisk or whatever. "It *must* be true." And then the supporting text of the Compact with Phineas started branching out in different directions, or more accurately, the text remained the way it was but the way people thought about it started branching out.

It fell upon the horns of Mack B. Goat to steer the program through the rocks and shoals of human thought. As the conquests of Alexander the Great splintered into three successor empirettes upon his death by friendly fire, so too the Goat Protocol needed to divide into original, western, and eastern components.

Some of you may remember the time before, the longest of longs ago, before Meetup and Linkedin, before even the fax machine. It wasn't easy to coordinate travel and meetings between continents. Mack picked a remote, but central, location for a rendezvous of the inheritors of Phineas, one each from the Latin and Eastern churches and one from the Judean Exilate.

The Tsaghkahovit Plain in central Armenia was home to a discovered fortress and Temple compound which also contained what amounts to a fortune cookie factory: "doughnut-holes" were stamped with an assortment of seals and, presumably, drawn out at random from a bag, revealing fortunes. Armenia was formally a Christian nation at this point, but the old Temple, even though it was of pagan origin, was given a pass. It seems that everybody likes tea and cookies.

When they were done with small talk, tea, and the formerly sacred munchkins, and a mini debate about the meaning of the fortune received by Celsus, the Roman, about whether he will really 'learn something new' today, Mack addressed the three Priests; Eastern, Western, and Hebrew. *"Gentlemen, please. Hayk, Celsus, Gedalyah. You're all educated men, dedicated to sanctity, holiness, God. The Anointed HAS come, the Anointed WILL come, the Anointed was Cyrus, was David, will be a descendant of David, IS a descendant of David, is Jesus. Jesus is Homoousious. Jesus is Homoiousious. Hayk, really. Can ANYONE besides you spell or even pronounce those words? Use them in a sentence?"*

Celsus, the tall Roman spoke, "Announced. Born. Preached. Was killed. Was raised back up. That's all. I agree with the goat. What is the purpose of these words you made up?"

Gedalyah, the equally tall Hebrew, grandson of Phannias, the only democratically elected High Priest, took a turn. "Just wait a *heleq*. Simon and his Zealots are still fighting. Twenty-one Roman Legions, can you imagine that? A bunch of farmers and herdsmen holding out for years against the largest fighting force ever assembled. Can you imagine that? That doesn't show him to be selected by God? But not only God, Simon has the backing of Akivah and the academy at Yavneh. These are the people who *invented* messiahs. Suppose he wins, suppose he's declared, suppose people start popping up out of the ground?"

Hayk was as argumentative as the other two Priests combined were tall. "If Gedalyah's Simon is really the Messiah, we won't need you, Mackie, will we? Why will we need goats if Heaven has descended upon the earth? The best course of action, it seems to me, is to do this my way. A rigorously established expiation mechanism for believers, goats to clear the sins of everyone else."

"Hayk, as smart as you are, we goats pre-date your fancy Greek words by far, they even pre-date the whole Greek language! What good does it do today for an abandoned wife, a neglected child, a beaten ox, when who knows when the Kingdom to come will actually come? The goats are for the people, so they can live in peace today, not for when they're dead. Then you can take over, fine. Gedalyah, the Israelites must follow the law, and following the law results in good outcomes, fruit grows on trees, no plagues, no famines, justice for the weak? Yes?"

"Yes, of course," the Judean answered, "leaving corners of fields for the poor to harvest means no one goes hungry. Worshipping trees didn't accomplish anything."

"And you, Hayk and Celsus, the saved now act a different way than before they were saved, yes? People should be helped, fed, healed? Your Jesus violated the Sabbath, in a synagogue, healing a cripple – not a dying man, but a suffering cripple—to heal him by the Grace of God in public? What is the meaning of that story? Could it be anything except that nothing is more important than to relieve suffering?"

"Well, um, yes…" said the Roman.

"Yes, but" started the Armenian.

"Butt me no buts. Butt, get it? I'm a goat. Let the goats do their job, and the three of you get to be in charge of what bad stuff gets cleared. Deal?"

CAP aNd NAN
ON THE ROAD, THE PRESENT

Nan was getting tired of the county music on the only radio station they could pick up, and opted for conversation. "So, Cap, tell me again why it is that you do this?"

"What, you mean accompanying a charming companion on a drive through primeval forests on the way to a bi-species ecumenical council?"

"No, hitch-hiking I can understand. Why do you spend your time trying to get people to do good stuff? Wouldn't you like to settle down with a *Madame Chevre*, have some kids—oh, now you've got me doing it—build a life for yourself that doesn't involve getting rides from strangers?"

"There are four reasons I do it. First, I can. Second, somebody has to. Third, I get absolutely no end of amusement in knowing that it takes a goat to teach good manners to the pinnacle of creation."

"And the fourth reason?"

"Bl*@t it. Oh yeah, there's a fourth reason. If I gave it up, somebody else might give it up, and so on, and eventually we wouldn't be able to have these conferences. No more frequent flier miles for us."

"It's a good thing I don't know where to punch a goat to let him know he's being a ninny... So, will you be presenting anything or speaking or organizing or whatever in Kalispell?"

"Nan, I'm a goat who hangs around bars and race tracks. What gave you the impression I was an academic? I do stuff. I'm not really that big on thinking about it. I'm joining with The Roofers and some of the other Indy goats to register our missions together. The Roofers are mainly Irish Goats, and they're keen to clear the Massacre at Smerwick. They came over to the first North American Conference after the Potato Famine. There's always a danger of us getting eaten during hard

27

times. Of course, there's more mission opportunity as well. Then again, North America was still pretty much virgin territory and may have been in need of a helping hoof. We generally work out what the best courses of action are."

"Roofers? Smerwick? Mission?" asked Nan.

"Missions are what we do. We get people to do good stuff to make up for all the bad stuff. To keep the... Well... Let's just say it's to keep the whole enterprise going. This part gets a little complicated. That girl in the bar? The wood chip enzyme lady? Her project could potentially prevent one mid-sized oil war and keep about 5,000 people a year from choking on tailpipe toxins. That is, if the money you gave her and her own stick-to-itiveness can get the project out the door. If it isn't stopped by the... well, the "other side."

The Roofers took it in hand to make sure kids didn't fall of roofs or out of windows or things like that. It was in the Bible somewhere, the Israelites were coming from their desert tents into Canaan, where they would have houses, and had to be told to put fences on their roofs. Very touching story, lots of wisdom in one little verse. And Smerwick. Well. As I say, I'm not an academic and I don't know who hated whom or why, but it was a medium-size massacre in Ireland, and the Roofers want it cleared."

"Okay. Mission. Roofers. Smerwick. But what is this 'Other Side?' This truck ride is starting to sound like a Webflix Original Series. I feel like something's going to jump out of the water at us when we pass by Moses Lake."

"Trust me, the world doesn't need monsters to be dangerous. Human beings do a good enough job on their own. It's true, our little pre-historic superstition has become organized, bureaucratized, even bowdlerized, some would say. There is status to consider. Perks. Power. The desire to have one's position be recognized as correct and acted upon. That's just normal for human affairs.

"But while the Homo sapiens part of the deal is being bowdlerized, it seems that status and power are infecting some of the goats. Human frailty is becoming, well, I guess you would call it Bovidized. That's us. Bovidae. Goats. Each of the Priests running the show comes with theological and cultural baggage. And now the goats are starting to think that way as well."

"Okay. So, there are a bunch of Priests, what, with an organization chart? A business plan?"

"It's always safe to give a goat classified information, you know. First of all, we just eat the paper. After going through four stomachs, no one is going to reconstruct anything. The system is easily an order of magnitude greater than the best shredder rented by Enron. And second of all, we don't blab, we bleat. And there's nothing

I've told you on this trip so far that you won't find out as my facilitator once we get where we're going."

SOPHIA
THAT TAMARISK PATH LED TO
BUREAUCRACY, THE PRESENT

Priests with organization charts, oh my. How did we get to this point? Eventually, that would turn out to be me getting the project to that point. And I'm supposed to be the wise one who should know that reality can't be organized in a chart, a table, or anything like that.

Under the compact with Phineas, things were easy. Whoever the high Priest was would select an appropriate candidate from the associate Priests. Appropriate meaning someone not particularly ambitious and could keep his mouth shut. The Goat Protocol was definitely an off-book operation, and the fewer the number of people who knew about it, the longer it was likely to last.

Two weeks before the Israelite New Year, the designee would camp in a field outside of Shiloh. Back then, all of the participating goats could pretty much walk from wherever they were from to Shiloh. Israel is in Asia, right next to Africa, and just a kick, leap, and bleat from Europe. The goats would tell the young man what they had accomplished that year. The High Priest kept a large cloth tent sheet rolled up and stuffed in cubby hole in the Holy of Holies, the one place no nosy Levite would take a chance entering. Every year, the designee would spread the sheet out on the field; goat names were in a column on the right-hand side and years ran in a row across the top. As he heard the tales, goat by goat, the Priest would mark the corresponding box, goat and year, with a score.

If a goat's cumulative score reached a threshold, the goat would be released and sent to a remote pasture owned by the High Priest's family. No goat from that land could be used as a sacrifice, none could be eaten. They gave wool and milk, and boys came to learn how to care for goats properly. At the end of the week, the Priest would count the scores for that year and decide if a massive, terrible act, or perhaps two or three smaller acts, possibly less terrible, or even a single bad act, could be stricken. That simple method lasted over a thousand years. Even during the Babylonian Captivity, there was a Priest stationed near Shiloh disguised as a farmer.

But then the Compact branched out, with Gedalyah, Hayk, and Celsus. And it kept branching.

Now any person ordained as a Priest, vowing to accept the maintenance of an Order of Service and deemed to be an acceptable intercessor between congregants and the Divine, and who is willing to take on the Bovid Cause of the struggle between bad and good, is eligible to participate. The presiding Priest is always a descendant of Gedalyah, and it took an awful lot of bleating to keep that franchise going.

There is no formal organization of Cohens, descendants of Aaron, the brother of Moses, of the family of Levi. The Cohens in any synagogue congregation bless the members every year on the Day of Atonement. Throughout the year, they are called first to read from the Torah. They accept the required five silver coins for redemption when any local Jewish woman has a first-born son. But they have no authority.

Their primary job, as it turns out, was to keep their family name, at least in the Hebrew version of their names, if not their local-language names. It turns out that one of the early Israelite Priests had a mutation on his Y-chromosome, which has passed down from generation to generation. In any Jewish community, anywhere in the world, a high proportion of the men identifying as Cohens has this genetic signature.

Of men identifying as Levites (descendants of Levi but not of Aaron), a somewhat smaller proportion has the signature. For the rest of the Jewish men in any tested community, the signature will show up at an even lower rate. This is true for Syrian Jews, Yemenite Jews, American Jews, Mountain Jews isolated for centuries, and even for the Bubba Clan in southwest Africa. These folks have an origin story of being descendants of Arabian territory Jews who migrated south after the arrival of Islam. They have been Christianized now, but they still maintain the Y-chromosome signature distribution. The notable exception is the Ethiopian Jewish community. By 16th Century

Rabbinic decree, when they were "discovered," they were ruled to be the lost Tribe of Dan. However, the historical record has them as African natives who were converted to Christianity but decided to become Jewish instead.

For general purposes, this establishes Jewish communities everywhere as having a more or less common ethnic origin. But for the purposes of the Goat Protocol, it allows a "kosher" Cohen to lead the circle of Priests. The job of whoever is the Jewish Priest is to accept the deeds initiated by the goats.

There is another member of the circle who is also a descendant of Aaron: A Greek Orthodox Priest. This man's ancestor was Iomtov, a Hellenized Jew from the Greek city of Delos, and a Cohen. The line between Judaism and Christianity was a little loopy and squiggly at that time, and it would not be uncommon for followers of Jesus to lecture in synagogues. Iomtov invited the proto-evangelist home for the Sabbath meal, and converted that day, and his great-grandson wound up as a Greek Christian Priest.

It took a lot of fancy hoof-work, but some orders of the Greek Orthodox Priesthood were open to married men, and somehow it was made sure that a descendant of Iomtov would always be in one of those orders. And now, whoever that may happen to be in any year, that descendant is designated the Lieutenant Priest, with the final authority to declare that any particular bad episode has been cleared by the work of the goats.

Going down the line in seniority, the next four slots parallel the College of Emperors of the later stages of the Roman Empire. A serving Priest from the Greek Orthodox or Russian Orthodox church bears the title Pontifex of the Augustus of the East. A Priest from the Coptic or Armenian church serves as Pontifex of the Caesar of the East. A Roman Catholic is Pontifex of the Augustus of the West, and a Latin Right Orthodox Church Priest is the Pontifex of the Caesar of the West.

Continuing downward in seniority, the group dedicated two Anglican Communion slots, one for the Church of England and one for the rest of the Anglican communion. Currently, these spots are reserved for woman Priests, and a good thing too, as we shall see. The ninth spot is held by a Buddhist Priest; although low in seniority, everyone else tends to defer to him on questions of awareness and suffering. The remaining three in the circle have observer status: a native shaman, or the closest thing, on the continent where the meeting takes place, and two neophytes to see if they have what it takes to do the job.

And that's how we got a bureaucracy. There's no chance of advancement, so there's no jockeying for position. And no nepotism or opportunities to be seduced by bribes, contributions, or favors. The only currency is getting one's own positions on bad and good, and what to do about them, advanced. One redeeming feature is that since the entire enterprise is kept secret from everyone, including each Priest's denominational hierarchy, there's no point in any individual Priest shilling for his or her own branch's position. Saves a lot of time and wasted diplomacy. But it's not for the faint of heart: if you enter a world of people concerned almost exclusively with theodicy and deciding between good or bad, go in armored.

NAN and CAP
ON THE TRUCK IN MILITIA TERRITORY

Cap spotted the road sign first. *"Welcome to Idaho, Nan. In about two hours we're going to be making a little stop. There's an opportunity to good to pass up."*

Nan was oscillating between the existence of talking goats and her job. "Really, Cap? I have a schedule to keep. Where and for what is this stop?"

"Really right back at you, Nan. You don't think a talking goat is a little more important than a piece of paper? Or just forget about the talking goat thing. What's more important, keeping civilization from self-destructing, or people getting t-shirts that say 'I FROZE MY BUTTE OF IN MONTANA'? And besides, have you noticed we've had a tail wind the whole way from Weed? And that no one is really paying attention to how fast you're going? This is not a one-sided relationship.

"We need to make a stop in Kellogg. Actually, the stop could probably be anywhere along I-90 until we turn off for Kalispell, but before I was—you know— sent away, we used to get Kellogg's cereal as treats. Anyway, there may be some folks there who can be...well...redirected. Turned around. That's double points, you know. Gets me one step closer to the petting zoo."

"Petting zoo? What, do bookies bring their kids? It's nice having a talking goat and all, and I'm happy to participate in something which is, and I'll take your word for it, a 'good cause.' But why couldn't I have just given a lift to one of those academic goats you were talking about? Then it would be just me and him and a bunch of papers in an Office Depot report cover. I have to admit, I'm a little nervous about the people you hang out with."

"Petting Zoos are the goat version of the 'sure and certain hope.' Only they actually are petting zoos with families coming to say hello, and chaffhaye and ivy to

eat, and maybe some Kellog's cereal. It's the end of the line for us when we've completed our missions. We get to live out our days being loved. And by the way, you don't have to be an academic goat to do research. We see stuff and we know stuff and we're pretty good at putting stuff together. Some of us like the field and some of us like to peck out tomes on a keyboard—specially designed, of course—with our noses. I've even tried my hoof at... Well, enough said about that. Goat security, I may have mentioned that."

"Oh, so you're a closet academic, is that it? What did you try researching? Let me guess. Ethics of state lottery games, marketing to the poor, funds siphoned off to who knows what budget item black hole? There's a mission for you."

"Even without the security restrictions, I can't really say. It's pre-publication. It would have to go to virgin anonymous reviewers before anything could happen."

"Not even a hint?"

"Well, just because you were kind enough to give me a ride, I'll share some generalities. The Goat Protocol, increasing goodness to remove badness, started well before Bible times. It was actually inserted into scripture by a deal between a Bronze Age scapegoat and an Israelite High Priest. There's no harm in telling you that, most of Scripture is syncretic—brought in from older sources—anyway. The deal between the goat, I-AM-WHAT-I-EAT, and Phineas, the Priest, was, on one side, to establish some permanence, structure, and authority for the project, and for the other side, to maintain some level of control of what might be a not-strictly-monotheistic phenomenon.

"That may or may not have been a good idea, but now we're stuck with it. So the question comes up year after year: is there a reason to continue refereeing multiple games with a single rule book? Are all the games really the same? Are all the rule books actually the same book? Or is there one with a valid signature? That's the question I'm researching. But when I research something, I do it by figuring the odds. That's how I work. I had absolutely no advance knowledge that Socks would win that race, but as sure as I know a kid'll eat ivy too, wouldn't you, I could calculate those true odds".

"Cap, if there's a signature you could point to, wouldn't that kill faith? What possible hope could one have of Heaven, or of an afterlife of any kind, without faith? Miracles occur on a regular basis, but after the first time, no one has since come back."

"Well, first off, MY afterlife will hopefully be in a petting zoo. But as for you folks, that's not what people want when they think of heaven, anyway. They want answers. People want to go to Heaven so they can find out why the Christmas puppy got hit by a car after only six months. Or where Mommy went to. And we're coming

up on Kellogg. Find somewhere to park the rig near the cable car station, I hope you're not afraid of heights!"

"We're taking a cable car ride? How much do they charge for a goat ticket? And why are we doing this?"

"What I'm looking for, by design, isn't obvious from the surface level. I have to go above the surface to see it. Whoever controls the high ground controls the battle, you know. And I'll be free, by the way. There should be an internet café in town somewhere, type up and print out a realish looking letter from your 'therapist' listing me as your emotional support goat."

"Do I look like I need emotional support?"

"Truth to tell, this whole trip, I haven't heard tweet, text, or call from a boyfriend, and you a good-looking woman and all that, spending most of your time as a hermit in your rolling cave. You don't even listen to your CB radio! Maybe you should accept a little support. The alternative is for me to climb, but that would set back your schedule even more."

"Support letter it is, I guess. And were you telling the truth when you said you couldn't see inside my head? We only just met yesterday, what gives you the idea that I'm a hermit?"

"Just guessing, based on a calculation of the odds…"

"I think someone mentioned a while back—on that CB radio you say I don't listen to—that the Fairbridge has truck parking in the back. We might have to spring for a room, though. Any more horse tips, Nathan Detroit?"

36

sophia
FACEBOOK VIDEO FODDER: GOATS USING SLIDE RULES. FODDER, GET IT?

It is said that when Archimedes, the greatest engineer to have ever viciously ridiculed a design proposal, died in the second Punic War, it was at the hands of Roman invaders. He was sketching out a geometric construction in the sand when the Roman soldiers came upon him; he asked them not to disturb his circles, and they killed him for his impudence. Either that, or for his geometer tools, which must have looked fancy and mystical enough to fetch a price. Plutarch wasn't sure, and you never will be, but I know the truth. If you think a 75-year-old graybeard advancing mathematics in the sand is something, you should see a dozen goats doing calculus with actual calculi and hoofmarks in the dirt trying to design a flying windmill.

Bert the Goat and his nerdy crew had determined that Chevy was wrong, and instead of a kite, the project would be better with a very tall, rigid, tetrahedral structure—like a pyramid, but with three sides. Then determined that it couldn't be built in time for the Great Assembly, and even if it could, it couldn't be transported anywhere. It would have had to have been built on site, but that would spoil the surprise. Then the project was recast as proof-of-concept prototype, in which any requested design features could be scrapped as long as the thing itself worked.

It certainly couldn't be stratospheric; the FAA and the EPA and the rest of the alphabet soup would, well, have a cow—a bovid cousin, of course—over that. They wouldn't get to justify using silver, which has much less resistance than copper, they wouldn't be able to demonstrate the advantages of generating electricity at 30 degrees below zero, and they sure wouldn't have the solar tower feature, so it couldn't even be called a scale model. It would just be a butt-ugly (there I go again) prototype. But by Capricorn the First, the Great Goat, by his horns and by his hooves, they would get Chevy his kite.

Bert and his awkward bunch got their facilitators to arrange a huge, old barn in Cut Bank as a fabrication facility and got to work. That's one of the good things about Montana, folks don't really stick their noses into other peoples' business, even if it looks like they're seeing goats operating metal stamping equipment. There are certainly a lot of goats around, and you never know what they could get up to.

The autogyro concept was invented about 50,000,000 years ago by an enterprising tree which would eventually evolve into today's oak. In addition to being able to peel open a little of an oak seed pod and stick it on your nose, the pods are aerodynamically evolved to fly far away from their trees using something now known as the autogyro effect. Unlike the powered autogyro seen in Mad Max, oak pod "wings" are impelled by the breeze to spin and generate lift.

That's what the Bo & Bert prototype will do: the impellors will be spun by the breeze, lift will be generated, the kite will go higher and higher where the wind is stronger and stronger and the impellors spin faster and faster and start generating electricity and sending it back down the line. This was originally a concept by Australian professor Bryan Roberts born during the energy shortages of the 1970s. But the Chevy & Bert production version would eventually be rigged to carry a siphon allowing hot surface-level air to the frigid stratosphere, generating more electricity by tapping the flow, and, in principle, slightly cooling the planet.

TAICH
THE LONE GOAT, TIMELESS

Meet Taich, one of the longest-serving goats in the project. And by longest serving, I mean he hasn't, on parchment at least, cleared enough badness to merit a trip to a petting zoo. He doesn't mind. He believes in one good inspiration at a time, even if it only benefits one person. He's been at this since before people had the capacity for bad acts on a truly massive scale and is therefore more familiar and comfortable with the old-fashioned way, one at a time.

He may also be the smartest of the flock. Instead of walking up to people, seeing if they can hear him, and then introducing himself, he waits behind a hedge and sees who responds to his voice while passing by; apparently people are a little more likely to hop to when they hear a voice in their own head as opposed seeing a talking animal. And that's a good niche for him, too, since he is one of the very few Pygmy Goats in the project.

Taich has gone from "Hey, why don't you help that fellow get his cart out of that rut!" to "What's the matter with you, are you going to let someone that old carry a box that size?" to "Are you just going to watch or are you going to help that lady change her flat tire?" And in the neighborhood of every hedge Taich hides behind, politesse and civility seem to spread. One getting-yelled-at at a time.

Someone at the top may have a use for a small, clever, seen-it-all talking goat.

CAP and NAN
EXCELSIOR MEETS ESTO PERPETUA

There it was. Silver Mountain. The familiest of family vacation spots, best night skiing in the Rockies. Apocryphally, it was so named because when it wasn't winter, if you looked at the leaves of the trees on the mountain, and they were silver, it would rain soon—an updraft effect. But I know the real story: It's named Silver Mountain for the same reason Leif Erricson named frozen Greenland Greenland. Real estate promotion.

Cap was a little miffed at his reception. *"Why do you think nobody wanted to ride in the gondola with us? Doesn't everybody like goats? We do a lot of funny stuff and we're very expressive."*

"Perhaps the next time we do something like this, you can follow my rig through the truck wash. Would you like your horns waxed and your hooves steam cleaned?" asked Nan.

"Okay, I get it, I get it. Bl*@ting olfactory oppression, that's what I say. Let's set up by that picnic table, and then we'll see if we can coordinate you holding the binoculars to my head while I'm scanning."

"And what is it we're looking for, again?"

"We're looking for something that doesn't want to be found. So we look for the absence of something. You know what, let's put you to work. You take the glasses and spot for me. Just look for what's missing and point me to it."

"Field. Barn. House. Another field. School. Wait. There's a driveway that just kind of disappears into some woods. Oh, looks like it's leading up to a playground? Hmmm… that's some funny playground…"

"Okay Nan, hook me up. Let's take a look. That's it, and it isn't a playground. It's a training ground. Good spotting, Nan. Let's get down and have

a little talk with these folks about what it really means to protect individual liberties, and whose liberties get protected, and from what."

"Cap, are you proposing what I think you're proposing? We're going to walk into an Idaho militia camp and try to convince them of something? How exactly would you feel on a spit being rubbed with Scotch Bonnet?"

SOPHIA
PLANNING FOR THE EVENT,
KALISPELL, THE PRESENT

Now that we have a bureaucracy, meetings must have agendas, and an agenda-setting committee.

NORTH AMERICAN CONTINENTAL GREAT ASSEMBLY
Kalispell, Montana, United States, July 2017
Committee Members Present:

- Father Theodosius Costello, Pontifex of the Augustus of the West
- Pastor JoBeth Berger
- Father Yiorgos Stephanides, Lieutenant Priest
- Father Daniel Yossarian, Pontifex of the Caesar of the East
- Oh, and me. Sophia.

As the junior member, Pastor JoBeth booked the conference room at the lodge—a woody affair, to say the least, with plenty of glacier photos so stunning they actually seemed to make the room colder. Pitons, ropes, ice hammers, and other glacier-climbing stuff was hung on the walls. JoBeth ordered the catering. It was a good thing that the Presiding Priest usually didn't serve on the agenda committee; it could be hard to get kosher food in some of the far-away places these meetings were held.

JoBeth took care of the housekeeping part of the meeting.

The towering, yet graceful, woman rose with a notebook in one hand and reading glasses in the other, pencils in five colors still on the table. "Usual stuff to open the Assembly this year," she began. "Convocation, That's you, Dan. Hope you have something

42

electrifying, and that you aren't going to use this as an excuse to lobby about not clearing Adana or 1915. Again."

"I've learned my lesson," said the darkly handsome Armenian. "Although I would like to see a Truth Commission or a reconciliation or something before those get cleared. But we each have our jobs and we should let each other alone to do them. As a matter of fact, I actually do have something literally electrifying. Bert Goat got a message to me that he and his crew were cooking up a little something with Chevy, and that project does have something to do with electricity. I'm guessing they've got something cooking for resource wars. He was a little short on details but he says when we see this, we'll be flying high."

Our Lieutenant Priest doesn't usually involve himself with the intricacies of the doing of good; his job is the clearing of bad. The Greek, round as a gyro, raised his hand. "Are we going to mention the Mormon thing this year? They do call themselves Priests. Are they to be excluded because they have too many Priests? Is it the homoousian versus homoiousian thing? That wasn't a factor for my ancestors, or for the people of our revered Presiding Priest. They changed their entrance requirements, isn't it time we changed ours?" No one wanted to answer. If everyone is a Priest, is anyone a Priest?

The Catholic spoke up, then: "One of my friends in the field got word to me; she thinks Cap is also going to have something, well, metaphorically electrifying. You might want to leave room in your address, Dan, for something, well, shocking." He looked around at the faces. "The goats don't hold a patent on bad puns."

"Friends?" asked JoBeth, "You know you're not supposed to be spying on the goats. This is their project, we just make it look like we're doing something official. They do the work, we do the parchmentwork."

"Spying? Begorrah, me?" said Ted defensively, laying on the brogue a little thick. "I think a compulsive gambler goat should be monitored, that's all. And I was helping, arranging a ride for him to Kalispell."

"Compulsive gambler? Cap?" Yiorgos was practically foaming at the mouth, although it may have been the tzatziki sauce. "He can out calculate even the most boring actuary on the planet. Literally. Before Cap, people used to take out life insurance policies on strangers and then kill them. Cap was able to get Mammon worshipers to see the link between ethics and math, with both of those fields winning, along with the rest of the population. I cleared the Santa Maria School in Chile for that. Compulsive? *Fila mou to kolo.*"

JoBeth, as usual, stepped in to defuse the situation. "Reverend sirs. Can we agree that while Cap may be obsessed with numbers, especially those that involve risks and rewards of unknown outcomes, he is NOT a compulsive gambler. And can we also agree to just let the goats do their job? Onward to other business. Would you each please present your reports on the guest list, seating chart, and transportation?"

ΛδVΙCΕ ϝor τhe ΝΕΟΡhγΤΕ
THE PRESENT

Two Priests were sharing a kettle of tea and a box of those little finger-peel oranges that always seem to come from somewhere far away, and generally in or around biblical territory. Father Arlyn De Jesus, Father by consecration but not by looks – he barely needed to shave—was nervously fingering the rosary in his pocket. He thought he had broken himself of that habit before he entered the Seminary. But there was a lot to be nervous about.

"You Jews have a saying, don't you? Know before whom you stand? Here I am, standing—well, sitting—before a man with a 3,000-year-old genealogy, literally a direct descendant of Moses' brother. As they would say where I come from, I'm hangin' with the matantan."

"Relax, kid. Until six years ago, I was a civil rights lawyer, I did voting rights cases, redlining, anything not on the square. Never got the big break, the big case. Never got my name in anything but local papers. But then this came along, and it's like I have my own personal Star Chamber to redress everything I came up short on. By the way, the whole line is 'Know three things: where you come from, where you are going, and before whom you stand. From a stinking drop, to a place of dust and ashes, and before the Lord God.' I never liked that one, there are much better lines from the same book" said Arphaxad Coen, the Presiding Priest.

"May I ask how you got the name Arphaxad? Of course, I've read the name in the Bible but never met anyone with the name." This was Father Arlyn's nervous attempt at small talk.

"I come from a very large family, and all of the mothers preferred biblical names and it's our tradition to not name babies after living relatives. By the time I came around, all the good names were taken. I've grown rather fond of it. It's not a Hebrew name, its original language may be lost to time, and no one can agree on what it means. That made me an International Attorney of Mystery, I guess. Anyway, are you ready, kid? You're risking de-frocking and eternal damnation for being here and participating in our little State Fair. I hope you've got the right amount of brandy in your relish."

"Brandy in the relish? Is that a Yiddish or Hebrew thing? I thought you folks preferred schnapps."

"Neither. It's an old movie that hinges on things being judged. *State Fair.* Pat Boone was the star. Do they have Netflix in the D.R.? You should stream it, very instructive for a musical comedy. And just for the record, Schnapps *is* brandy. Tell me what your plan is."

"I'm going to take notes. My cousin decided not to go to the Seminary after all, but the Priests knew he had something. They scratched together some funds and pulled some strings and sent him to Wharton. Two things a diocese needs are people with good business sense and people with good business sense who have well-paying jobs. He told me that when you start out, keep your mouth shut and take notes. Everyone appreciates it, it looks like you're eager and helpful. So I'm going to take notes. Not just take notes—I'm going to be an amanuensis."

"And you think putting your impressions next to what was actually happening will help? Help you? Help us? It probably will. You're fresh eyes, you might spot things we take for granted. But the help will be for next year. I shouldn't tell you this, but the scoring of the neophytes is based on how closely they come to the scoring of the regular members. If you want in, play it conservative, but if you spot something we all missed, speak up. It's more important that the grading of the goats is correct than if one or another neophyte gets in. And who knows, if what you've got is really, and I mean *really* good, the group might give you credit for it. Probably not, but hey, we're in a situation of engaging in an academic exercise with talking goats. Anything can happen. Do you have any questions?"

"Well, just one, but it's embarrassing."

"Go ahead, kid. In the past five years, I've seen it all. Shoot."

"Do you really do the Vulcan Salute under your prayer shawls?"

"Once a year, kid. Like clockwork. Netonic clockwork, but still clockwork."

sophia
APPARENTLY, IT REALLY IS
ALL ABOUT THE NUMBERS

Vatican City is not the world capital of religious intrigue. And from what I've seen, being present at the creation, so to speak, even off-world religious intrigue takes a back seat to what could go on at some of these Continental Assemblies. It was time for me to roll up my sleeves and get to work. I stepped out of the shadows and started talking.

"Teddy. JoBeth. Georgie. Danny. You know the Big Guy doesn't like interfering with the project. He rather likes what evolved with the goats. But you know me. I cry without and yell in the streets and in the malls. And though it's never been my role to be a manager—I'm more or less a consultant—you've got to get the numbers up. Seriously. And seriously up."

JoBeth spoke up. "I don't suppose it would do any good to say that if He wants the numbers up, he can make them go up? He is the Big Guy, after all, isn't he? And now you're going to say that it doesn't work that way, right? Give us some Scholastic shyte or discuss the incompatibility of omniscience and omnipotence? How's that for an act of prophecy?"

"You're right, it doesn't work that way. This is baked into creation. We've had our shots, and most of us—I mean all of us, going back forever—missed the shots. And if the score tips the wrong way before...well, just before."

I knew this was going to be unpleasant. Better give them a reminder of who I am. "Listen to your sister, folks. Don't be afraid of fear." That should do it. "Ted, so, now that you've bent the rules with your 'friend,' tell us what you know about what Cap's doing. If you don't mind."

No one can hem and haw like an Irishman. "So. Yes, well. Ahem. It's like this. It could wind up as a complete dogmatic overhaul. Who can tell how that will be received? The whole meaning of being a believer could change. It might not involve suffering anymore. It might be, well, ahem, hmmm, shall we say, um…easy"

Irish. Suffering as a virtue. "Making things easier is a bad thing? And by the way, whose dogma is going to be affected? Collectively, you've all got so many different ones. Spill it, Teddy, me lad. Before I start uttering and crying out. Or worse, singing." I dropped an old silver wagon wheel dollar on the table to get an A and started in. "How does it go? Oh, the village cripple he was there, he couldn't do very much, so he lined the girls against a wall and…"

"Sophia. Please." That was JoBeth, a true believer in the sinfulness of profanity. Not much for laughter, either. But she could sure cater.

"Okay." Theodosius Patrick Costello, revered father, now minus the accent and the vocal dissembling. "Discoverability. Cap is going for discoverability. I don't have any details at this time. That's all I know."

"See? I told you, listen to your sister and don't be afraid of fear. This is good news. Greater market penetration," I said, wondering how GMAT words got inside me. Will wonders never cease. The Big Enchilada in the sky is going to love this.

I continued, turning my authority dial up to eight. "Trust me, my cloistered companions. It's not pretty out there. Whatever your particular eschatology is, it can change. For the worse. Cap gets the pre-reception spot on day one. Sort of a 'cap'tive audience, one might say. Any other surprises you think are losers? Speak up. Don't be afraid of fear."

Dark Armenian eyes flashed. In other circumstances—very other— I could imagine the traffic along my pudendal nerve rivaling anything the Long Island Expressway has to offer when my Toozik is around. "At this point, Bert Goat, his crew, and Chevy are goat-only. By horns, hooves, and teeth the goats are doing the assembly. I mean that literally. They hooked up with Bo and his facilitator, the computer game cheater. Jim, that's his name. More of a protégé than a facilitator, I think. The kid rigged up a waldo system that the goats can operate.

And don't ask me about the carbon source for the monofilaments, you don't want to know.

This was new. Maybe I should be afraid of fear. Would this count? Goats have never done anything bad. Well, depending on one's perspective, that is. "Dan, you're the Lieutenant Priest. You're in charge of deciding whether or not to accept this. How are you going to play it?"

"I'm going to give them plenty of vine," Dan said in that sexy, vaguely pentatonic voice. Sometimes I wonder what it would be like to actually have the pieces I look like I'm supposed to have. "But I'm not going to wait and see if they hang themselves. I'll have to debate myself as to whether it counts if they get someone to reproduce the kites and do something with them. I heard that when Chevy isn't busy throwing dogmatic fall-off horns into the works, he'll operate on Resources Conflicts, but within the guidelines. Not that goats have guidelines. Chevy is fighting a handicap. I don't know how closely you're following the situation up there, but…"

I interrupted him and my daydream. "I'm down here now. I read the papers. Even though they're not on paper anymore. You want to talk about miracles? You read an article, hit read more, click the graphic, and when you try to get back to the page you started on, like magic, it's now completely different. Perhaps miracle is the wrong word. But anyway. I've seen the Children of Adam put up a dozen, maybe more, cracker jack solutions for resource wars. And every time, someone gets a grant, gets funding to continue research, gets a subsidy to sell at market price, and that's it. Again, magic, the market drops to make whatever the idea was that year 'uncompetitive.' These people. You know, I told Him this would be a bad idea. But does he listen? And if someone actually gets close to rollout. Then they have to pay to prove that their deep-water partial-vacuum desalinater straw is cleaner than someone burning lignite."

Dan again. That voice. "Are we on the same page, Sophie? Will the QA department pass it through?"

"We haven't been speaking lately," I told my Toozik. "But perhaps there's an understanding among the horned."

STAN
SYMPATHY, COURTESY, AND TASTE

Please allow me to introduce myself, I'm a man who loves to baste. Geez, I get a lot of mileage out of that line. But that's not me, that's the other guy. Me, you wouldn't look twice at if we were both seated around a conference table, except maybe to wonder about how long and bushy my hair is. You'd probably guess Silicon Valley freak. You might even be right. There's an awful lot of valleys that have an awful lot of silicon in them.

"Hello, Stan," I greeted my fellow Original. "Butting into the narration? Butting. Hah. Still funny. Isn't this outside your brief?"

"Sophie, Sophie... As much as I would love to get you outside of your briefs, I'm here doing my job. Two jobs. One, if you're going to tell the story of the goats, not that anyone is going to think it's not just another magical pseudo-realism middle-grade wannabe, I'm going to assure that it's a quality product. That's what I do. I assure quality. The second job is just for me. I don't want to be left out. You know how childish I can be."

"You're right. I could use your help on this. Thanks for coming," Sophia said.

"Always a pleasure to assist a fellow Original, my dear. Perhaps we can discuss it over...what is that these folks do? Oh yes. Discuss important ideas over alcohol so they can ignore any of the bad points of those ideas. A drink. Let's talk over a drink," Stan offered

"No time for that Stan. Do you really want to help?"

"Mais oui, mon petit chou..."

"Oh yeah, I forgot, you have charms. What's your next line? 'Vous etes une ange descendu sur terre?' If you really want to help, go back over the first fifty pages and make sure all the commas and periods are in the right places. Just keep in mind that I'm a little more Original than you are."

"That may be true, but your job is pretty much done, isn't it? And my job, as the Quality Assurance Officer, is finding the kinks in your job. We all have our jobs to do, Sopheleh."

"A gunnery sergeant can ream an artillery officer, but he's still got to ask 'How high?' when the snot-nosed 2nd lieutenant tells him to jump."

"I'm not the other guy. We're supposed to be on the same side. Can't you give me a hint about what's coming up?"

"All you had to do was ask, no need to try to get into my pants. As long as you brought him up, how is our unreconstructed rebel doing?"

"Actually, not so good. He's depressed. I tried to get him to lose the wings; after all, he's no Cherub. I told him to modernize, get a social media platform. He said nothing was any good. The base line empathy level has been steadily improving, giving him far fewer opportunities. But in the places where local empathy is declining, nobody needs him pushing them to do whatever it is they think Mr. Big told them to do. Sad, really."

"Sad? I guess that's in the heart of the beholder. I'm going to tell you what to look out for, but I want you to clue me in if you think our shining friend is up to anything. Deal?" I asked.

"Always a pleasure to do business with you, Sophia. In or out of your briefs."

"Three items for attention. Someone is going to be presenting discoverability. I'm neutral on that, it's really up to the Priests to take care of. One of the Priests has a line on one of the facilitators on a mission. That's bad, but the Priest claims exigent circumstances. I don't buy it." Sophia shook her head. "And Bert and his crew are operating capra solo. Supposedly there's a human connection, but it's kind of like putting one solar panel on the roof of a car to run the radio and saying you've got a solar-powered car. This could be trouble."

"Thanks, babe. I'm not going to worry about Bert and his group. We knew all along that they'd follow the Slide Rule rather than Mr. Big rules. And I can tell you that keeping tabs on an ongoing mission is a lot more common than you know. But discoverablity is a problem. It will throw the whole 'faith' thing off." Stan considered. "But the goat project began well before faith. Did animists need faith? Maybe it was

Enoch—I-AM-WHAT-I-EAT—who threw the project off the rails making a deal with Phineas. Well, I've got a paycheck to earn and slim pickings to earn it with. So long, and don't take any wooden nickels! Do people still say that?"

NAN and CAP
GOING TO MONTANA SOON

"Okay, Nan, I think you're coming up on your ten-hour sleep break. Let's cross the line into Montana. I'm not sure how much of what I told those folks in Idaho is going to stick, or whether or not they've got people looking for us. Not likely, but we're so close, I'd hate to chew up the carpet padding now." Cap paused. *"It's a goat thing, you wouldn't understand. The first town with a motel is Saltese, the Mangold Motel and Store. I hope they have truck parking. You're going to meet your counterpart. That should be fun. In fact, you should call him no; tell him to meet us in Saltese."*

Nan's curiosity was acting up. "Why do I have a counterpart? How many people does it take to drive you to Montana?"

"See, it's starting to be fun already. You're the facilitator, you're keeping me safe, getting us where we're going, and you're getting comfortable with the idea that things aren't always what they seem, but also some things are exactly what they seem. I hope that makes sense."

"Let me parse that last line, Cap… Okay, yes, some goats can indeed talk to some people. But goats, preachers, liberals or editorial writers, bad and good are just what they seem? Not bad for a country girl truck driver. So what about this counterpart?"

"Siegfried Tynan. I'll answer before you ask, his father is an opera singer. You're a facilitator, he's got a Mission. That's his job. We'll meet up with him tonight. I understand he's very good looking, for a human. You should call him and tell him we're coming. Tell him you're a friend of Cap's. He'll know what that means. You want to see research? This guy is all about research. He used to steal Global Outdial to get into the EDGAR database and the Xerox PhD dissertation database. Just for fun. You'll love Siggy."

***

The pain of having it withheld, the temptation of having it offered.

Part of Quality Assurance these days was monitoring mass communications, especially broadcast, commercial television. That was the kitchen in which assaults on cultural mores were baked. And the instant Stan saw an episode of *The X-Files* in which The Men Behind the Scenes would meet in an apartment on East 45th Street in New York, across the street from the United Nations, he decided that his terrestrial headquarters had to be right there in Tudor City. Stan did it all, the dark wood paneling, the antique globe, the bar with nothing but scotch. Nick would be visiting him for the first time.

"Nick, come in. Of your own 'free will,' of course." Stan gave himself a case of the chuckles every time he used that line. "Oh, brother, have I got a job for you. You look awful, you know. Maybe this will cheer you up. Or maybe you should just go home, I know for a fact that the Big Guy would welcome you back." This was Stan as he is when he's at home. Very rare.

"'Brother.' Nice of you to grant me rank. Don't you think I already have enough to do?" Our nephew, Star of the Morning, at least until Velikovsky ruined the story for everyone. Pointy tail, pitchfork, and all. Our nephew Nick.

"Really, Nick. So many people are busy pursuing the Evil Urge themselves, how many are left for you to pursue, effectively or not? I've got something good for you. This is my assignment, but it's right in your wheelhouse. You've got a 50/50 shot at getting a win, and either way, my job is done. Deal?"

Nick is an expert at deals, screwing people. He took his time to answer. "And if I lose? As you said, your job is done but as for me... How about this? Give me a fallback, something in, say, the 70/30 range."

"Nicky, Nicky. You want an 85% shot? Is this a basketball personal foul free-throw? What happened to you? You used to be able to just sniff the air in a room where someone's been and know what buttons to push. What's wrong? Is it social media? Mid-life crisis? Low-T?"

"It's your dime, Stan. Deal or no deal? Or do you want a rematch playing ping pong with waffle irons? Settle it that way?"

"Deal. There's a man from Antioch..."

sophiᴀ
EIGHT MILLION WAYS TO MISUNDERSTAND

The man from Antioch, Father Gregory. He just showed up one year. And for all anyone today knows, 'one year' might actually have been the year one. Our Pontifex of the Caesar of the West. Stan was legitimately able to assign him a 70% temptation score because, at some point, he did switch sides. But as for properly being tempted, well... Little Nicky will have his work cut out for him.

But who knows. I'm Wisdom, not The Shadow. I don't know what evil lurks in the hearts of men until it leaks out. This would be a game I want to see, but would hate to be played. Of course, it's going to get played. Stan and I know exactly which of Nicky's buttons to push.

Even before Nick gets to test Father Gregory, just his warm-up is going to be torture. And poor Bronwyn, she's to wind up as a doe on the highway trying to get her fauns back to the safety of the tree line.

BRONWYN
SOCIAL MEDIA. SOMEWHERE IN THE CLOUD

[Nicholas Rigel]: Will you accept my friend request? I've read some of your posts. I've known two women in similar circumstances and was able to help both of them. I may be able to help you.

[Bronwyn Higgins]: Sure. Bet I know what kind of "help" you're offering. And I'm not available for that sort of thing. If you've read my posts, you'd know I am a priest.

[Nicholas Rigel]: That's definitely not what I'm about. I can find your kids. Get them back for you. Husbands who abscond with the kids fall into a pattern. Wife messes up, husband gets scared for the kids, poof. The "poof" part is my job. Walking back the cat, the mechanics of the poof can be worked out. That's all it takes. And my software—still beta right now—walks the cat back.

[Bronwyn Higgins]: You should be ashamed of yourself, preying on crime victims, taking the money from people who have already lost their hope.

56

[Nicholas Rigel]: Who said anything about money? It's a free download. Just read and accept the terms of service so I can use you as a success story to promote the commercial version.

Answer all of the questions to the best of your ability. Then the program crunches that into the best leads, reports to me, and then I do the leg work. The algorithm saves hundreds of hours of private investigator time. Since it's software, it doesn't need per diems or expenses! Bronwyn, you can get your kids back. If it doesn't work as promised, you can dip me into a vat of boiling oil. I'd deserve it for getting your hopes up and then dashing them. Whaddaya say?

[Bronwyn Higgins]: What was that download link again?

Nicky is such a sneak. In the old days, when people tended to value their immortal souls, there would be an impressive contract—in hand-drawn calligraphy, on high quality parchment—attesting to the transaction and awaiting merely a signature in blood. The tempted one had a chance to grasp the seriousness of the situation and back out, although no one ever did. Who would think to look for a "you are selling your soul in exchange for the use of this product" clause on page 14, paragraph 9, section G?

Nicky was working fast. Bronwyn got a knock on the door two days after she filled in the form from "Nicholas Rigel's" software.

"Mrs. Brownie Higgins?" The New Hampshire state trooper struggled over the Celtic name.

"Not so sure about the Mrs. I haven't seen my husband in six years. I'm Reverend Higgins, what can I do for you, son?"

The young smokey quickly switched gears from talking down to talking up. "Reverend Higgins, there's been an accident, I'm sorry to say. And you might be seeing your husband for the last time. We're going to need you to come to Berlin to identify your husband's body.

I'm sorry, ma'am. Reverend. And he had custody of your two children?"

Bronwyn had to wait until her heart retreated from her throat and went back into her chest before answering. "Custody? Dick stole those kids and left six years ago. Were my kids in the accident? Are they okay? And was he living in Berlin all this time? Just over the mountains, and you people couldn't find him until he died?"

"Don't you think it's wrong to speak ill of the dead, ma'am? Reverend? Especially so soon?"

"What? No." Bronwyn shook her head. "His name was Richard. Dick."

"Oh. Sorry. Ma'am. Reverend. They were living sort of off grid, just outside of Shelburne, edge of the forest. The family was going under the name Julian."

"Julian? Really? Telling. Are you sure it was an accident? You should go over that car very thoroughly."

"I can assure you, Reverend, there is going to be a full investigation and a thorough report. Some of us suspected something funny was going on, but the kids seemed to be in good shape, had their shots, went to school, and jurisdiction can be a little funny on federal land. Your daughter, Fiona, told us your name. She only had minor injuries in the accident. She and David are in Androscoggin. David should still be in surgery."

"It's Daffid. Surgery for what?"

"I'm sorry, Reverend Higgins. It's his spine. The doctors are doing what they can. We should know more when we get there. The duty nurse is going to text me if there's any news. But you should know something about your daughter. Richard—and, um, Daffid. They were bringing your daughter back from rehab."

"Rehab? She's 14! And I thought you said everything looked good!"

"It did look good. She hid it well until she couldn't hide it anymore. I'm sorry. At least she completed her program."

Bronwyn was a priest. A Priest who was due in Kalispell in a couple of weeks. She tried to recall if she had ever smelled an actual rat before. Would she know what one smelled like? Two kids. Both found two days after the Encounter on her profile. And two weeks before the Assembly. Nicholas Rigel. Rigel is a star, isn't it? Has to be visible from somewhere some mornings, doesn't it? "I'm sorry, Officer, um…"

"Tetrault, Reverend. Sergeant Dominic Tetrault, at your service. Shall we start out?"

"Please. Call me Bronnie. I'm very likely to be crying on your shoulder much of the way over the mountains. But I'm going to have to check something on my computer real quick. Won't take more than three shakes of a lamb's tail. Do people still say that? Four, tops."

Control-F is wonderful thing. I'm going to recommend to the Big Guy that he should put it in the next release. You know, say, if you lose your keys. You could just say "Control Eff My Keys" and your keys would flash blue, or yellow, or any good contrasting color. The releases are coming fast and, well, not exactly furious. Sort of. Well. And the Guy upstairs doesn't take criticism well, fast and sloppy. It took almost 2,000 years between the time Democritus proposed the theory of atoms and when a new release was needed for when people started looking inside the atoms. But then it was less than a hundred years till we had to release a version with quarks, the stuff that was inside what was inside atoms. And then maybe twenty years until we decided on a blind alley release: string theory. That won't last forever.

Bronwyn quickly found the soul selling clause and then froze, leaving Sergeant Tetrault on the porch. If she went to pick up her kids, the contract, if it was a contract, would be in force. If she didn't go, would the contract still be in force? How could she not see her kids? She was waiting for this day for six years. And she didn't even have the advantage of disbelief all the other tempted had: she was deeply immersed in at the least practical metaphysics, and at worst, an actual theology with souls and a soul stealer. And talking goats. I'm going to go, she decided. See them. Have them get their mother back. Yes, there's a contract. Of sorts. But where there are contracts, there are lawyers.

NAN and CAP
LUNCHEON IS SERVED

Cap's ears and tails stood up like a kid hearing its mother's call when he saw his Missionary. *"Siggy! You made it! Meet Nan, my facilitator, trucker extraordinaire…"*

Seigfreid looked a little older and wiser than the last time he had seen Cap. "Cap! You have no idea how much I missed your nagging and pushing. After you hit the road, I realized it was inspiration and motivation."

"Nice to meet you in person." Nan was staring at the researcher's pocket protector. She was too young to have ever seen one, except maybe in a movie or a Dilbert comic strip. Was she seeing a baby slide rule? And a four-color pen? Cap noticed the stare.

"I told you he was something, didn't I? Suis generis. Hey, Sig, what's that hanging out of your pocket between the Napier's pinky phalanges and the Terry Collins pen?"

"This?" Sig was fingering some beads on a chain. "It's my rosary, how do you like it? As of two days ago, I am now a Roman Catholic."

"Hmmm… I got the impression from Cap that you were all about data and analysis, not the religious type. Was I wrong?"

"Nope, this is news to me as well. Spill it, Sig. What made Mr. Naturalism turn to the smells and bells?"

"Naturalism, of course. I'm going to get us some chow. In case you don't like the local grass, Cap, I brought along some treats for you. This is going to be a whole dinner's worth of story." Sig tossed over a burlap bag. "It wasn't easy getting chaffhaye. And here's some Chex mix, of course. Nan, any comestibles your heart desires can be found in the store up front. As long as your desire is a sandwich. What'll it be? Head cheese and swiss? Cappicola and pimento? Rye, white, wheat, bagel?"

"Let's see if they can make my favorite. Rare roast beef and Muenster with coleslaw. Are we close enough to the Pacific Northwest for them to have sourdough bread? Maybe a Portuguese roll? Maybe two sandwiches. Trucking is hungry work. I leave it in your newly-blessed hands, Sig. And hey, this place looks old enough for them to have Coke in glass bottles!"

"One First Supper repast coming right up!" Sig could never resist a good parting line. Cap took the opportunity to sound out Nan on his friend's mental state. A Roman Catholic?

"Nan, I know you've never seen Siggy before. You don't know what's normal for him. But you're a fellow human. Is the kid alright? Or does he need to have some work done? This conversion thing is a surprise."

"I've seen my share of folks coming out of tent meetings with that come-to-Jesus look. This isn't that. I think he had a fright, a big one. But he said he's going to tell us the story, why don't we wait and see what he says?

"This is too important to get blown up. I've mentioned the fact that there's another side, haven't I? Hostel 1, 2, *and* 3 *plus* I Spit on Your Grave *and a sprinkling of Korean horror movies don't add up to the fright the Other Side can engender. Usually they stay out of goat protocol business, unless they get a hint that an envelope is getting pushed. Then they seize their chance. And there are two envelopes being pushed this year. Siegfried Tynan is one of them. And I also heard through goatnet that there may be something not quite kosher in the State of Montana. The Quality Assurance team is scary enough."*

Nan took a beat to check her make-up to hide the possibility of her face turning completely pale. She thought she was helping out an important project. Had she done something wrong? "Well, he made it here in one piece, didn't he? And Catholicism isn't exactly the other side, is it? I mean, you've got Priests and all running the show, don't you?"

"Priests. Yes. Each and every one of them involved in something in direct contravention of their orders, denominations, and vows. Except for Jampa, of course. Our moral compass from the high plateau of the far east, here now in the high plains of America."

Cap and Nan took a think-break, and came back to life when Sig showed up with the food.

Siegfried laid out the food, such as it was. "So it's like this. Apparently, a member of your fraternity of the interstate is tardy in delivering to Saltese, Montana. Salami, cheddar, onions, tomato, and mustard on Wonder Bread toast. But it's good salami. Somehow it made its way here from Katz's Deli in New York. This is an age of miracles and wonders. That was one long-distance haul. Oh, and they had, of all things…birch beer. Local microbrew, made from local birch. Care to say grace, Nan?"

A question that brought it all home to Nancy Unger. Not only wasn't she in Kansas anymore, she couldn't be sure she was inhabiting the old, familiar, Earth she grew up on. "Grace? To whom? To Cap? He's the objective miracle, and he's not jerking his hoof up to the sky. Now that we know there's a level, can we know if there's a higher level?" Nan paused. "You know, that does look like a good sandwich. Let me wrap this up. The Priests running this show, most of them are heretical, aren't they? At least technically? Okay. 'Grace.' That's it. Whoever wants it can take it. Let's eat. Why are there a bunch of dogs staring at us from the tree line? Is it the kosher salami?"

SOPHIA
AN INTERULDE

Domestic dogs and domestic cattle seem to have shown up at around the same time. It's not exactly symbiosis; dogs and people would do just fine without each other, but together each side gets far more accomplished than they would alone. I'll let you in on a little secret. The Guy in the Sky has taken a liking to the relationship. He spends a fair amount of time matching dogs with their people to guide them, watch over them, protect them, and teach them.

This isn't some hippy-dippy, earthy-crunchy, new age barnyard byproduct. When you take a dog into your home, it immediately establishes a defensive perimeter with three cordon lines: you'll never not know when a potential enemy is approaching. They eagerly seek to be useful; they know their "status in the pack" depends on it. There are free-climbers (well, not the near-vertical ones) who trust dogs to pick the best routes.

When you see a purportedly lazy dog napping on a couch, notice that she has located herself to have sight lines of all of the entrances to the room. Partnering with a dog allows you the opportunity to observe just how little it takes to put a fellow creature into a state of ecstasy or bliss. And to learn the lesson that if you want to play ball, at some point you have to let the ball go from your mouth.

For people rescuing dogs, it's always an open question as to who is rescuing whom. And amazingly, people trust these apex predators with their most treasured possessions: their children, their livestock, their homes. To borrow a phrase from "Father" Guido Sarducci, there are miracles and there are card tricks. Joshua parting the Jordan for the Israelites was a card trick—He put the Priests and all of their stuff upstream a couple of clicks. The Jordan is not a major artery of maritime intercourse; a passel of guys standing in it would have stopped the flow for a while. But two killers making a useful and long lasting partnership? Positively Divine. You can take that from me.

CAP and JUBILEE
LUNCHTIME

Dogs protect sheep, cows, and goats. And since Koen the goat, although he didn't notice his escort, dogs have shown up to provide security whenever a goat's mission, or the Goat Protocol as a whole, looks like it's getting rocky. Now Jubilee, a stunning girl Decker Rat Terrier, perfect cow pattern, black on white with fawn trim, ears proudly up, nub oscillating madly, found herself a rock to stand on, since Ratties need to climb and need to be higher than anyone else. This locally-assembled posse accepted her as pack leader *pro tem* since Ratties are the most loquacious of breeds.

Cap walked over to the rock, and he and Jubilee sniffed and licked each other, and offered the traditional greetings.

"Hi howaya, niceta meetcha, d'jeet?"

"Hi howaya, goodta seeya. Gophers. Had couple roaming green place where two-legs hit balls stick. Balls no good, no squeak, not soft. Tugboat daddy teach Tugboat find ball, daddy trade ball green paper trade yum food. Good way come. Get here now good. Bad come. Goat two-leg pack danger. Me come. We come."

Cap respected canine precognitive abilities. He never took a position on whether or not it was just a good multi-sense processing algorithm or something else. During the Green Revolution, he had a woman on a Mission in the early days of radar weather forecasting. Cap tested her meteorological prognostications against the dog pack's, which had apparently showed up to fill this specific need. When the math hit 93% of the dogs' prediction rate, Cap gave the young graduate student the high-sign to push the math up the chain.

"So what's coming?"

"Many bad. Red Goat Two Legs. Two-legs fight two-legs."

Cap wished his friends' communication skills matched their future-telling abilities. Red Goat Two Legs could only be Nick, of whom Cap had only heard rumors. Two-legs fight? That had to be bad. The project depended on some degree of unity. By the time Cap trotted back to the motel deck, the lunch party had begun to grow. Could this be the much bad, starting so soon?

Cap had met Cockeyed Jenny once before. It would be hard to think of her as being part of anything bad. She was the sweetest goat ever in the history of the project. She did have a handicap, though. She was born with a lazy eye, very disconcerting to the people in her village. It was rumored that she was selected as the scapegoat not because she would have been the best at clearing away the bad, but because people wanted her gone. All of her Missions were subject to extra scrutiny.

Never the less, she was on her way to clearing the massacre at Al Andalus/Granada, and getting a trip to the petting zoo. When Cap had met her, he reminded her that Leah, who also had a lazy eye, was the foremother of most of the Children of Israel, and under the Compact with Phineas, she should be accorded special status. What was she doing here? And was that an AMC Gremlin with a trailer in the parking lot? At least no one would ask the driver where the other half of his car was, he was towing it behind him. And could that be a '72 Eldorado Station Wagon making the turn? That could only be one man's car. But of course, who knows who drives what in the high plains?

"Jenny! What a treat seeing you, better than a mouthful of chaffehaye!" Cap greeted.

Jenny was, as usual, acting shy, looking down, absently scratching the ground with her hoof. *"Hi, Cap! Long time. Getting ivy in your travels? Chex? We were pulling in for lunch when we saw you. Slim pickin's for Mister Thang for lunch, though, although Nan says the New York salami is pretty good. How did it get to Saltese, Montana? That's gotta be a story."* She nodded to her facilitator. *"Cap, this is Mister Thang, by the way. Mister, meet Cap. Watch out for that old goat. Whatever he says, it's a probable 12 to 7."*

Cap looked at the Missionary, at least he assumed Mister Thang was on a Mission for Jenny, up and down. High fade, high cheekbones, high shoulders. High yeller, someone might have said last century, if that someone felt like risking getting his teeth knocked out by one of those giant hams. Hamptons Shinicock? Connecticut Pequod? One of the two.

"Nice to meet you, Mister. You're in good hands with Jenny. And it looks like she's in pretty good hands with you."

"Same here. Jenny mentioned your kindness to her, but I didn't think I'd get to meet you until Kalispell. Jenny mentioned you were a gambling gamboler. I sold my share in the Nutmeg Casino as soon as I heard this little beauty talk, and agreed to go on her Mission. Reckon talk isn't the right word, is it? Goatcast, more like. My people traded the spirits of nature for fleecing the palefaces. That only goes so far before it gets revolting. How 'bout you? Where'dya pick up the bug?" Cap's olfactory alarms kicked in; something was off. And then he saw—could it be?—a mezuzah around a neck that had to be size 19, at least.

"I wouldn't exactly call myself a gambler. More like Mr. Spock, when he would rattle off those ridiculously precise odds for Captain Kirk. If I happen to calculate something and there happens to be someone to take the action, and I happen to have a facilitator, well, maybe it's good for a demonstration. Take yourself, for example. I had you at 85% for mixed Native American, within 50 miles of Block Island sound. And your chain? Bar Mitzvah present? Did I read something in a paper I was munching on about 20 or 25 years ago, the Chief's Bar Mitzvah?"

"Sorry to bust your streak, Cap. No, that wasn't me. And it was a Bat Mitzvah."

That's why his nose was sending up flares. *"So, you're facilitating for Jenny and on a Mission? That's some juggling act."*

"I'm some juggler, my ungulate friend. I can do even numbers, no sweat. But this worked out well; the Mission is a road show. I'm Black, Indian, Jewish, and trans. Anywhere I turn up, someone is going to hate me; maybe hate me two, three, or four times. But the flip side is that I have quadruple the number of people to inspire. The Mission is to turn the whole self-esteem thing inside out. Instead of handing out trophies to everyone, I want hated, shunned, and bullied people to act AS IF. You know, from that movie, Boiler Room. Act AS IF. Drip esteem from your skin, make people smell it.

"Look at Vin Diesel in that movie. No one knew what he was, black, white, Italian, Jewish, straight, gay. But he sure looked like he had self-esteem, and he sure got plenty of work. Of course, after *Pitch Black*, they never let him actually act again, but that's another story. If a scared little injun girl could turn herself into this, anyone can do anything. And the crabs in a bucket thing? Turning that upside down. From now on, the crabs that reach the top of the bucket are going to help the other ones up and over. Frogs in hot water? From now on, those frogs are leaving the pot as soon as they break a sweat."

Cap took an instant liking to Mister Thang. *"Welcome to the team, Mister. Looks like the Guy who Lives over the Shop made Jenny cockeyed so she could see around the twists and turns. Good job, both of you."*

Just then the Eldorado made it up the drive, creaking, groaning, and hissing to a stop. Nan and Cap both ran out to greet it, Nan Waving and shouting "Father Ted! Father Ted!"

Cap took a beat. *"You know him, Nan?"*

"That car could only have one driver. Father Ted, my basketball coach at Saint Agatha's. And Siggy has been waiting for you to come back so he can relate the story of his conversion. It looks like he's going to explode if he doesn't get it out. And now he has an audience, and I'm sure Father Ted is going to be happy that there's one won for the Gipper. And my cold sandwich is getting colder."

Jenny and Cap took up positions on the grass, of course, joined by Mister. Nan took Theodosius to the table on the deck to join Siggy. Siegfried Tynan, despite his parentage, turned a little shy in public speaking. Maybe he should sing the story. He went for the cliché and cleared his throat.

"Cap, of course, knows the background. I was in the field when I thought I was flipping out and heard a goat talking to me. Literally in an actual field, by the way, doing a sterile-seed audit for Monstranto. Not a noble task, I can assure you. I genuinely enjoy putting the pieces together. Solving the puzzle. Catching somebody doing something really wrong, finding the second set of books. Maintaining corporate control of the food supply? Not so much. Maybe it was because he was a numbers goat and I'm a numbers guy that we hit it off."

Siggy cleared his throat again.

"Cap asked me if I went to Sunday School, Hebrew School, Bible Study, anything like that, when I was a kid. I said I did, but I quit when one of the teachers repurposed the Bed of Procrustes story to describe what the people of Sodom wanted to do with the messengers staying at Lot's house. You know, the bed where if your feet are too long they cut them off, or if they're too short, they stretch you on a rack. I was a precocious kid, I knew what was going on, and the class just lost all credibility with me.

"Then, he asked me if I was a numbers kid before I was a numbers guy, and I said yes, in fact, I was. Then he asked if the numbers in

Genesis meant anything to me, the ages and stuff, and I said, yes, I always thought there was some kind of pattern in there somewhere, that the numbers had far more precision than most of the numbers in the rest of the *Bible*.

"Then he asked me if I wanted to do something for good, looking more closely at what was in the *Bible* instead of working for the machine. I said sure. He gave me a couple of sports tips, and emailed me more every few weeks. Said it was his version of the McArthur grant. Then I got a result."

Mister Thang got up off the grass and spoke out. "And that made you convert to Catholicism?"

"Absolutely not. Why pick Catholicism over any other Bible religion? No, this was recent. A, what do you call it? A Visitation."

Mister was wowed at the depths of Siegfried's recruitment. "You mean more of a Visitation than a talking goat?"

"Different. The goats are apparently pretty much like us. They want to do their goat jobs, take care of their families, have fun. It's just the four legs, no thumbs thing that's the difference. This was an Exorcist-class Visitation."

"Please, do tell!" Jenny and Cap bleated approval, stamped their hooves on the grass. Ted joined in with a "Whoot, whoot!" Odd to see that coming from a mackerel-snapper. Sig no longer needed to clear his throat.

"Well. As I said, much to my surprise, I got a result. Real deal. The days of creation are tracking something called the 'increasing metallicity of the universe.' Starts out at minus zip on day one, enough solid stuff to make planets on day two, enough nitrogen to make plants on day three. And our particular solar system? *Bible* has it on day four, two thirds of the way into the age of the universe, which is exactly what we now observe it to be. Day five has enough calcium, magnesium, zinc, phosphorous—all the stuff you get in the drugstore vitamins to support vertebrate life.

"And all those incredible lifespans? 920 years for Adam? 969 for Methuselah? C'mon. But oddly enough, they're tracking geology between the two largest volcanic super-eruptions ever experienced by people up till then, Toba and Thera, and the beginnings and endings of two glaciations between them. Plus plenty of technical details along the way we're only just discovering now.

"It takes a little work to lay it all out on a line, and I'll be happy to go into it with anyone who needs a cure for insomnia, but it's really there, a signature. A data set which could only be known, 2,600 years ago, by somebody who knew what time it was. If not God's signature, the signature of someone involved in the composition of the *Bible*, That someone being not a contemporaneous person. An objective demonstration that something about the *Bible* is, if not supernatural or supranatural, at least extraordinary.

"I code-named the project Job3822. Since the signature could only be read by someone who knew what was going on with the universe and the planet, I used God's response to Job: '*Have you entered the storehouse of the snow? Have you seen where the hail is bound up?* By 1943, we actually have. We are the intended recipients of this message."

Nan could barely contain herself, and she was an expert at containing things and keeping them contained while moving at high speeds. "I haven't seen that even as click-bait on Facebook. What did you do with the result?"

"First, I thought, I needed to get it peer reviewed, have my calculations and stats looked over by people who do that for a living. Have my Hebrew interpretations gone over for reasonableness. See if it could fend off a charge of cherry-picking, or post-hoc analysis, or wishful thinking, or self-delusion. I can at least tell you there's no cherry-picking in this project. Remember Joseph and the divining cup? I wanted to find out exactly when on the time line physical, manufactured objects were used to tell fortunes. I had six databases at a time open. Finally, I found it. On the Armenian plains, a fortune cookie factory, roughly contemporary with Joseph. Can you believe it? A fortune cookie factory?"

Mister Thang couldn't resist. "They had Chinese take-out three thousand years ago?"

"Nope. But you could always send out for Lula Kebab."

It was Father Ted's turn for a good throat clearing. "Siegfried, what are you talking about? What does this establish? You can match any set of words to any set of anything else. What are you trying to accomplish?"

Siggy was tired of pontificating. The goats weren't the only ones who could play the pun game. He decided to use whatever genetic gifts his father gave him, and burst out into song, although he was pretty sure that the senior Tynan never sang any Broadway songs.

"Big bang... nebular disk, cleaving diff'ring densities
of plasma, a fluid.
Father, who do you think would do it?

Nucleosynthesis... of nitrogen
Father tell me this occurred when?
When did grass grow so green?
When were the waving palms seen?

Our beautiful moon, our warming sun
Father, when was the work on these done?

Selenium, magnesium, calcium carbonate
When were these here to make backbones straight?

So cold, began a journey frought, that
Warm animal coats were sought

Our cousins, rough,
but tender to touch?
Gone now but leaving their gift in us.

The warming sun, the ice dam burst, the water cold
Father, did we drown in days of old?

Drink the wine, bake the bricks, build the spire
Father when did we learn to aspire?

"Father Ted. It's 22 matches on three time lines unbraided from the 4004 BCE date everyone keeps yelling about. Cap, you can verify this. Four of the 22 matches have ranges too broad to put into a correlation calculation, but for the other 18, getting 16, 17, or 18 correct is what, 1600:1 against?"

Cap bleated his assent. *"He's right, Padre. He can't reject a null hypothesis but he's got something."*

Another phlegm adjustment from the Priest "And this has to do with your conversion? Your Visitation?"

"Folks, you have GOT to hear this. Much to my surprise, it turns out that this work is completely shut out of the peer review process.

71

You know what you would get if you mixed this research with ham?"

Mister Thang let out a bellow. "Cold spam is what you get? That what you're trying to say? Leave the puns to the goats.

"Okay, okay. I've done a 'close read' of a book. The close read led to a novel interpretation. The interpretation is backed by commonly understood scientific research, although much of that research only took place in the last 50 years. This isn't too surprising; a guy in England not long ago did a close read of Plato and found a hidden musical link to Pythagoras, everybody loved that.

"But I had the misfortune of doing a close read of a book in the *Bible*. What I did would commonly be called an exegesis. Super, there's a name for it, there's gonna be journals about it. Now, here's the thing. It used to be that people would study scriptural texts and try to string verses together to support their particular theological positions, everybody would get all excited and sometimes go to war with each other. It was a real mess. Still is.

"So now, what they've got is this thing called High Criticism. No God. No God, no wars. It's basically who wrote what, when, and why was it so important to ascribe what they were writing to an invisible man who lives in the sky. So, see, anything that was a prophecy, they would date the writing of it to **before** the thing being prophesized about, get it?

"No hocus pocus, no abracadabra, although those are both actually Bible-related terms, as I found out in my research. But no God, no God-ish or otherwise special thing allowed into the park. If my result is that somebody knew about high density plasma outside of the solar system's bow shock, or when and how we were doing the hey-hey with the Neanderthals, that's against the rules."

Cap started getting an uncharacteristic sinking feeling about this Mission. Uncharacteristic because goats need so little to be happy. As they say, "Who is rich? The one who is satisfied with what he's got."

"It's a science project too, any luck getting a real scientific review? Or what about those, whaddaya call them, Apologists? Folks who want to square whatever their text says with what everyone sees when they look around?"

"Hmmm. Now we're getting closer to why I have a rosary in my pocket. Crap out on one, dealer blackjack on the other. Believe me, I tried. What I got back was basically 'Take a hike, Creationist provocateur!" And from the Creationists? 'Get lost, atheist scum!' So there I am, all that work, looking like I'm going to disappoint Cap. And guess what happened next?"

Jenny, sweet as she was, was getting bored, quietly drawing caricatures of everyone in the dirt. *"It better be your Visitation. I can talk, I can read, but apparently my version of the software doesn't let me — what would be the verb? Academe? Academize? What happened next, Sig?"*

"The Devil came down to Nebraska."

Mister Thang couldn't resist. "What, Dick Cheney is well enough to drive out of his undisclosed location?"

"No, the actual Lucifer, in the flesh, or chitin, or whatever he's got going on for an exterior surface. I turned around, and there was this guy, shining in my living room. Lobster red. Looked like he used turtle wax to get himself so bright. Goat horns. Scaly tail. Wings! Can you imagine? I thought it was a prank."

SICFRIED
FLASHBACK

"Who are you supposed to be, the Devil? What's up with the wings? Lucifer is supposed to be an angel, not a cherub. Let me see you fly."

His jaw dropped a little bit when I nailed him on the wings thing, I could see he was missing a few teeth. Then he fluttered a little, actually got airborne, but lost a couple of feathers to my ceiling fan, and dropped onto my couch. "You okay there, chief? Can I get you something? Glass of water? Ichor? I've got a smoothie machine. Really, you don't look so hot."

With a couple of winces, creaks, and sighs, he managed to get reasonably vertical and drew himself up. "I am the Prince of Darkness, young man. You will accord me the respect that is my due."

"Personally, I'd rather you were the Duke of Earl, you're creeping me out,' I told him. 'You're in my home. I offered you refreshment, medical attention. Whaddaya need, chief? Cowering? I'll put my boots on so's I can quake in 'em, if you like. It's just that I'd rather not have to watch the EMTs trying to google diabolical resuscitation techniques."

"Young man, Siegfried, it's come to my attention that you are having a spot of trouble getting published."

"Oh, okay, I get it. You wandered into my blog, right? You're a self-publishing company, right? Nice trick. How did you get in? How did you manage the flying bit? If I dropped you off the terrace, would you make it down in one piece?" He managed to get his eyes to flash, sort of like a Van De Graaff generator with a loose connection and a shaky power supply. But it was still eerie.

"I can place you with one of the big five, kid. I've got somebody on

74

SCAPECOATS: THE GOAT PROTOCOLS

contract in each of those houses. All you have to do is sign. I hope you don't get too fat from snacking in Green Rooms. GMA, *Today*, *The View*, Kimmel. You'll still have to do the bookstore thing, can't be helped. Here."

He passed me what looked like a sales contract, literary representation in exchange for my soul. I wondered how many writers took the deal. But the functional wings…the eyes…the appearing out of nowhere. I knew there were talking goats, why not a two-legged winged one, the actual Morning Star here in my apartment. I did what came naturally to me. I asked him to excuse me while I got my lucky pen, and then came back with a fire extinguisher, the smoothie container, a can where I keep my loose change, a clove of garlic. One of those should work; apparently the can of change annoyed the, well, Hell out of him. And then after he was gone, I did the only rational thing."

SIGFRIED and the MISSIONARIES
BACK IN THE FIELD

Bleats and assorted "Which was?" remarks flowed over Sig, Even Tugboat and Jubilee chimed in with "*Red goat two legs bad bad bad.*"

"If you know that there is a real Devil, there can only be one course of action. I grabbed the feather from the ceiling fan and said. 'Alexa, find nearest Catholic church.' The feather burst into flames when it got within six feet of the baptismal font, waking up the duty Priest. I had him baptize me on the spot. My first confession took four hours. I moved next door to the church and I confess once or twice a day.

"Getting tight with the Big Five would be cool, but a Lake of Fire would definitely not be, well, cool. In any sense. Besides, the Assembly was coming up. Most of the Priests have doctorates and academic connections, there will be plenty of Missionaries and facilitators. If God, or whoever was hanging around, kibitzing, while the *Bible* was being written down, wants to be discovered, this would be the place to make that happen."

Jenny was the first to assimilate the story and its implications. She usurped Cap's right to congratulate his Missionary by walking up to Sig, putting her forelegs on his hips and giving him a good, solid lick.

"*I'm not sure how this is going to play out, but I think this young man has shown us an extraordinary level of both logical reasoning and resolve to follow through on that reasoning. Cap, you've got a winner there. He could not only handicap Pascal's wager, he could probably poke holes in some of Euler's as well.*"

Jenny let out her 'Bravo!' bleat, and then everyone rushed Sig. He was engulfed with hand and hoof shakes, back pats, and a 'Good show, old bean, jolly, jolly good show. Pity we lost Inja' from Mister Thang with a wink and a nod. Nobody doubted that Mister could, in fact, be anything he wanted to be. Even the dogs came around with licks, tags, and leg humps.

"Two-legs smart! Smart Two-legs! We keep safe. Trouble come."

The Irish Priest was last in line and whispered his congratulations to Sig.

"After lunch, after we're all squared away, come see me. I'd like to discuss this with you. Someone else will be joining us, I'd like you to meet him."

The Moral Hazard of Accepting Rejection

JoBeth not only had to organize the committee meeting, she was also juggling a publish or perish nightmare on her day job. She finished handling everyone's complaints about rooms, food, office supplies and wi-fi, took a walk outside, fired up her e-cig (her favorite flavor, cherry) and then returned to her room to face the email window on her laptop. She was soon to find out that *Yavneh Patristics*, thirty densely-researched pages on the influence of First Century BCE rabbinic authors of the Mishnah on First Century CE early church fathers, focusing on Moral Influence, was going to be rejected by the Tulsa Theological Review. As had *Ravena Nicenes*, by the assorted journals she submitted to. She rolled her mouse around to light up the screen.

"Gosh darn the day I was born" she said, reading the polite and appreciative, but ultimately negative decision of TTR. "And the lonely night I decided to play the academic game. What do these people have against Jews? Didn't Cardinal O'Conner in New York say 'Face it, without the Jews, we're nothing?' Didn't Aquinas use Maimonides, a Rabbi, as a source? Don't people want to know where their belief systems came from? What is it with Christianity these days? All they want from the Jews is to have them go to Israel and then die or convert during the Tribulation so Jesus could come back. Who do I complain to about this? I use whatever bloody style manuals these people want, whatever font, margins, type sizes they want, references as footnotes, references as endnotes, and what do I get? No. And no. And no again."

JoBeth began to itch, a sure sign of a pending panic attack. She decided to head it off with more of the cold Montana air, and bumped into Father Arlyn, the Dominican Priest. Dominican Republic, she reminded herself, she didn't know if he was a Dominican, a Franciscan, a Jesuit, or whatever. It was hard for her to keep them straight. She had to stop the itching, so she just started blurting out in a jumble, soon making a soft landing in front of the unsuspecting young Priest.

"All I want is for people to know why they believe what they believe, and what it means to believe whatever way they do. Is that so wrong?"

Arlyn started to itch a bit himself, and to display other signs of frazzlement. Then his pastoral training kicked in.

"Everything okay? It's JoBeth, isn't it? Mother JoBeth isn't the correct address, is it?"

That anchored the British Priest to reality. "No, you're right, it's Pastor or Reverend. But you can call me anything, really, just don't call me late for dinner!" Arlyn didn't get the reference. He was black, JoBeth saw, but not an American black. Probably didn't have to put up with minstrel shows and such.

"You look like you didn't get a date for the prom. It's never too late, care to dance?" Arlyn asked his smart phone to play a Mambo. At least that got her to smile. And then to dance. For a member of the clergy, she had plenty of rhythm and sway, some good moves. She toned it down a bit, realizing the unfairness: Arlyn was vowed to celibacy and practically still a boy, and she was not so vowed and very much a woman. It wouldn't do for him to think she was a cougar. Did they have that in the Dominican Republic? That probably existed everywhere.

Her first academic paper to be published, *War and Marriage in Tiwi Land*, documented the practice among a people settled in Australia for tens of thousands of years. Parents "betrothed" their baby daughters to successful hunters and warriors in their 30s and 40s. Widows in their 30s and 40s wound up with teenage men. Apparently, Animist influences on morality, ethics, and sacraments were okay while sources from other religions were not. Jo snapped into focus and realized what was going on.

JoBeth came back down to Earth. "Nice Job, Father Arlyn. You've pastored me down from the precipice. What was your grade in that class? Did you have to do an internship?"

"Due to the paucity of Priests, our Seminary has been grading on a pass/fail basis. And also due to the paucity of Priests, we all have extensive internships, fellowships, residencies, just to get the work done. So let's talk about your precipice…or do you not wish to cross dogmatic lines? Not that the line between us is all that thick. 'Thick,' or 'Wide?' English is a third language for me."

Had Arlyn's classes been properly graded, he would have received full marks for self-effacement, humility, and appearance of empathy.

"Wide or narrow if you're crossing the line, thick or thin if you're dangling from it. Is it easier for a native Spanish speaker to learn the Tridentine Mass? To read and write in Latin? I mean, easier than for someone from Cornwall? I never fear crossing lines, but I always do a thorough check before dangling. Arlyn, I'm looking for justice. Not only is the deck being stacked against me, every card is the queen of spades. Every two, three, or four years I would get a nice and interesting paper published somewhere, I was progressing along the tenure track, I had my church to run, I was happy, I thought I was making other people happy.

"And saved. Really. People saw my smile and believed that there was something good behind all of the mumbo-jumbo. But now? I keep expecting someone to come and hang a leper's bell around my neck. Most of the early Christians were Hellenized Syrian or Turkish Jews, on the secular side but still conversant with Rabbinic traditions and writings. Peter himself preached to the Jews of Antioch, and he was a big hit. But then something happened. All of the Aramaic versions of the Gospels are gone. Anything Hebrew is anathema. Ezra said, you have to read the law "with understanding." Why throw out that scripturally mandated understanding? Why is this still going on today? I **demand** to know what's going on. I demand academic justice.

"I know there's a mentor out there who can navigate me through this, where is she? I want to talk to whoever is in charge. I've worked too hard on this. And not only that, I can be deep in research or pondering or whatever, and then my husband will decide he wants to put the church accounts onto a spreadsheet but can't find the previous file, and I have to do it for him. Or his screen goes blank, switches to Chinese, whatever, I have to take care of that. I've not only been sandbagged, I've been hobbled."

"I'm sure the Anglicans are up on that line of reasoning. Be cheerful in your giving. Whom, is that who or whom, I can never tell, would you rather be? The one who can help or the one who needs to helped? But moving on. Is there something you've done wrong? Maybe something you didn't think was wrong at the time? And who are you blaming, academia or fate? Or something bigger? Is there someone or something you have to get right with? Is that the expression, to reconcile, to get right with? Why not make a list, like that TV show, where that guy, was his name Ed, he went around apologizing to everyone he ever offended. I don't know how it ended, our satellite dish was lost in a hurricane, and then I was in Seminary. Not much TV there. And even if there were, they make the Priests go around in threes, no one could agree on what to watch. Start small, work your way up, see if something changes. We're both in the goat project, this should be, what's the expression, ancient sombrero? Just pulling your leg, Reverend Pastor. Old hat."

"You never answered my question about your Latin, father. Simul Justus et Pecador."

"Very good. Righteous and a sinner both, eh? How righteous, how sinful? You're a professor, yes? You've taught many, counseled many as a Priest. It's your turn now, maybe, to be taught and counseled."

"Father Arlyn, the limit of my transgression is grumbling. To myself. Something is happening to me. I can tell. *Tulsa Theological Review* is modern criticism, I picked them specifically because they don't have the baggage of some of the denominational, the whack-job, or the political rags. Nothing will stop me until I get justice."

"Well, my unexpectedly good Mambo dancing colleague, during orientation it was mentioned that there is an opportunity at the Assembly to, well, address things. And that the addresses must be heard. Perhaps you will have your day in court."

"That's only been done once before, the results were quite ambiguous. But thank you for reminding me, pastor. Perhaps that's the way to go…"

The Third Man

The Montana Club was a carpenter's version of paradise. Woodwork exposed in the Alpine ceilings, wooden beams visible. A central fireplace; this close to the glaciers, it came in handy. A bar that could satisfy any tippler, imbiber, or out-and-out drunkard.

Theodosius was desperately trying to keep from sounding guilty. "Hi, Sig. Thanks for meting me in the Montana; I'm guessing this isn't your current preference of venue, if it even ever was. I just wanted to be out from under prying eyes for this; Canid, Capra, or Homo. And feel free to confess to me if you succumb to anything here, I am a Catholic Priest, you know. Say hello to my friend Stan, he's a sort of expert in the field of your current research."

Sig unconsciously fingered his rosary, but succeeded in suppressing his other 'tells'.

"Father Ted. Thanks for inviting me. I can't wait to try the bison burger. And at this point, I'd talk to anyone interested in my Mission. That includes the bar-backs and waitresses. Nice meeting you, Stan. What can you do for me?" Handshakes all around, and they settled in to study the menus and then ordered. Who'd have thought they'd have Dr. Brown's Celray Tonic in Montana? Stan crackled his knuckles and grinned like he couldn't resist grinning, and got down to business.

"So tell me, Mr. Tynan, and let me say I'm a big fan of your dad, being operatic seems to be my natural milieu. How sure are you of your results?"

"I'll pass along your compliments, of course. There are actually three components to be sure of. I'm dead sure of the math. Father Ted says you're an expert, I don't have to explain Pearson's R or the coefficient of determination to you, do I? Stories in Genesis, from Adam to Jacob, contain specific technical details pointing to real-world

82

events, and can also be dated because all of those folks have their lifespans charted out within the text.

"When you graph on one axis the textual mid-life date of Adam and each of his descendants through Seth mentioned in conjunction with or near a story, and the real-world dates of the events referred to by the stories on a secondary axis, the two curves are almost identical. To the extent that I've correctly matched story details to real-world events, the calendar information in Genesis is 95% determined by the real-world dating of the events alluded to, in spite of the fact that no one should have been able to know the real world dating when the *Bible* was being written.

"The same matching is true for the Days of Creation stories. Today, this is not hard to see if you take the trouble to look. Plants need nitrogen, right? There was an earliest time when there could have been nitrogen. Fire-baked bricks make snazzier and longer lasting structures than sun-dried bricks, don't they? There was a specific point when somebody figured out to bake bricks in an oven like pots. Mt. Santorini caused an agricultural disruption with fingerprints that can be found all over the world, right? Especially affecting the Southeastern Mediterranean, Yes? And that eruption happened at a specific time, right?

"Moving on. The currently observed upper limit for human lifespans is about 120 years, right? The Hayflick Limit? Same number as in Genesis? That's a decryption key written in plain text. Using that key shows that the Genesis numbers ARE the real numbers of when that stuff happened, systematically encoded. So yes. I'm sure of the math. For the other two components, one I can safely and happily ignore, and one I have no control over."

Stan was plotting his moves. "And what might those other two components be, if you don't mind my asking?"

"Well, Stan, I don't mind you asking, but may I ask what your interest is in this? Are you an agent? Publisher? University scout? Do they have those? Cars and girls as recruitment tools? Or are you a competitor? Are you looking for a co-authorship?"

"I don't think you could understand how great or important my interest is."

"Now you just sound like a nut. Ted, who is this guy, really? What does he want? I was literally ready to sell my soul to the Devil to move this forward. Poor bastard missed getting it by *this much*," said Sig, holding his thumb and forefinger separated by about the width of a quarter. "Your friend should start making sense presently or sooner. If I was able to handle the actual Lucifer, well…"

Ted went into is default hemming and hawing mode and the brogue popped back in.

"Steady on, laddiebuck." Laddiebuck? Do people still say that? "Stan here outranks your recent visitor. He outranks pretty much everyone. He's from Quality Assurance." For some unexplained reason, Sig had never been high enough in a corporate environment and had never sufficiently screwed up enough to interact with QA. He had seen survivors, though.

"Okay. But I'm watching you, Stan. And you too, Ted, you're vouching for the big shot. My objectivity can always be called into question. The thing that gets us out of the 16th Century and a planet that's 6,021 years old is the obvious observation – and it's an objective obvious observation, in my opinion, which doesn't seem to count for much, that the time line in Genesis is on *three* separate scales. Once the stories, the technical details, and the real events are sorted out on the right timelines, everything falls into place.

"Creation days for the history of the universe, decadents of Adam for the history of our culture, and a sort of murky undated scale describing the origin of, well, us. That's the part that people call Deuterogenesis, the second creation. So how objective am I in sorting out the time lines? How objective am I in matching details to events? I mean, if Abraham serves milk with lunch to strangers, it means that the Lactase Persistence gene mutation made it to the Middle East by that time, which it did. Straightforward.

"But the book also has a detail that has us living under a dome — a firmament. So am I being objective or subjective in deciding that our 'dome' is our solar magnetosphere? It serves the same function as described in the text, separating a fluid above from a fluid below. In the book the fluid is water, in the real-world match, it's high-density plasma. This is coming straight from the data being sent back by the first Voyager mission.

"I can talk for hours about that, but it still won't settle the question of objectivity. I mean, walk the cat back through the earlier texts. Gilgamesh's flood, the precursor of Noah's was rain-only. Noah's had groundwater flooding as well. And what is it that we observe today? When the glaciers started to melt, it began in Missoula, Montana, not far from here; gigantic trapped lakes bursting through ice dams. Shaped the whole Pacific Northwest. Who put that detail in while moving the story from one book to another? Every other cosmogony has an infinitely pre-existing chaos eventually sorted out by some god or other. Genesis has a zero point in time, as does the Big Bang. For decades, people rejected the Big Bang Theory because they thought it was a Catholic conspiracy. Well. As they say on TV infomercials, 'But wait, there's more!'

"Assuming that the correlation between the details and the real-world events is valid, setting aside my objectivity or lack thereof, we have a 'signature' of someone 'special' involved in writing Genesis. But what exactly is being signed?

"The subsequent books have lots of rules and regulations, many of which seem designed to address problems faced in the initial book, especially injustice and famine. Are they being specially authorized by this signature? Pentateuch rules for the harvest – letting poor people pick and keep some of your crops, not muzzling the draft animals, having to live in the field during the harvest – result in large amounts of mixed manure applied to the fields in Autumn.

"Today we know that results in extra nitrogen and better crop yields than just applying fertilizer at planting. Did they really do that? Did it work? Did anyone else do that? Who figured it out first? These are all answerable questions, no one has to rely on my objectivity.

"There are rules for epidemiology and public health, including washing, isolation of the infected, universal health care with a sliding scale payment system. There's even a recipe for soap and instructions to use it when washing utensils. Who figured this out first? Did it work? There are labor rules, including a day off, commerce rules, a division of doing bad stuff into crimes, torts, and breaches. Basically, a lot of the stuff modern, successful societies have today. But is this a subjective over-reach? My objectivity can be tested, as long as someone is willing to do the work."

"And the third thing?"

"Academic methodology. I don't have any. I'm not an academic. I find 'second sets' of books, which is what I did in this case, and what I was doing when I met Cap. So, I'm overly broad, I'm performing something called a post hoc analysis, I'm positing an effect without a causal chain, the list goes on. And that's just the overt criticism. I have it from multiple sources that no one will touch this for fear of embarrassment about entertaining the idea of something possibly God-ish involved in the composition of the Bible. As far as I'm concerned, they can all autohelicate."

Ted, as an Irishman, fancied himself a wordsmith. He had to ask. "Autohelicate?"

"It's Greek, Ted. A helix is a screw. Auto means by yourself. Would you guys like to hear a ghost story?"

Stan and Ted nodded assent, Stan a little twitchy, as if he were looking for a trap. Sig dived right in.

"This is what can happen when you get too close to the truth. This is the bizarre and tragic case of Dr. Elisabeth Targ. Elisabeth's dad, Russel, is a prominent physicist and also a 'parapsychologist' doing contract work for the CIA in 'remote viewing.' He was also a frequent guest on Art Bell's Coast to Coast AM radio show. We can say he is the original Man Who Stares at Goats.

"Elisabeth was a psychiatrist. I'm going to go a little bit out on the Electra limb here and say that Elisabeth wanted to do what she could to establish that her dad was not a 'pseudoscientist,' as he has been called by the 'real' scientists. This story takes place during pre-AZT days of the AIDS crisis and organizations would fund anything that might lead to a cure.

"So the younger Dr. Targ decided to make a protocol, get a grant, and research the possibility of 'remote healing' doing some good for AIDS patients. Her protocol didn't reach statistical significance, so she did exactly what I would have done if I were testing an audit hypothesis and didn't score a direct hit: she looked at the other metrics in the project and post-hoc'd one that actually did show significance and sought to move on with a fresh round of testing for the new metric of choice.

"For me, that's how I make my living, but, or so I've been told, that's a scientific no-no. But Dr. Targ went me one better: She moved beyond AIDS to a disease with medicine's worst recovery rate, a type of brain tumor called a glioblastoma. Anything that could move the needle on that would be welcome regardless of methodology. Glioblastoma is a very rapidly progressing disease but is asymptomatic for a long time, you're practically dead once it's detected.

"Dr. Targ decided to test this disease with remote healing, and she also died of it, despite penultimately putting herself in the position of remote healing subject. My opinion is that if anyone in the world had the brains, the balls, the resources and the support to find a valid parapsychological reproducible healing paradigm, it would be Dr. Elisabeth Targ.

"What we can't know is if Dr. Targ knew she had the disease before she started the experiment. Based on the timing of the disease's progress, it's doubtful that she did. I place this very public private ghost story somewhere in between dark irony and the universe not wanting to give up its mystical secrets but also wanting to state that in an emphatic and public way."

Stan looked slightly more nervous than he did before the story was told. Maybe 'guilty' would be a better adjective. Ted was the first to talk.

"Are you old enough to remember the original Odd Couple TV show? Maybe you caught it in reruns?"

"I would catch one every once in a while, they were always hysterical. They don't really make TV like that anymore, do they?"

Ted went on. "That's for sure. Felix and Oscar were dealing with an occultist of some sort and for some purpose, I can't remember what, but the occultist delivered one line I'll always remember: 'What you don't know can hurt you a whole lot.'"

"Exactly. So what don't I know about you guys, and how can you hurt me?"

"Siggy, Stan and I were wondering if you've considered the implications of your work. From what I've seen, I know your project is belief-neutral. But someone might get the totally unwarranted idea that there is 'objective proof for the existence of God.' That would upset everybody's apple carts. Would you rob people of their faith? You're a Catholic now, don't you have faith?"

Sig decidedly did not like what was going on, nor did he like where it was going. He pushed his plate toward the center of the table and stood up. Stood up both literally and figuratively.

"Faith? Belief in a concept on the credit of the teller. Ya know, when they put 'In God We Trust' on the money, it was a joke. The next line was supposed to be 'All Others Pay Cash.' Gentlemen—and I'm being generous in according that status to you both—there's a pretty wide gap between faith and belief. Our problem is that we do it to ourselves, individually and collectively.

"The solution is Stone Soup. Or Nail Soup; I think that depends on which side of the Rhine River you come from. It's just that simple, anything else is just an excuse to sound smart and important. As for myself, I sat down to play Pascal's wager. There was a shiner on the table and I got a peek at the dealer's hole card, so I took the insurance bet, and here I am fingering a bunch of beads.

"You know, the ten of spades is much blacker than the ace of spades. You should keep that in mind. We now have some tiny bit of information about the reality we inhabit, and I think that information should be shared with the rest of the folks on the plane before it augers in. And oh, just for the record.

"You are correct that the project does not constitute 'Proof of Divinity.' Almost all of the finding can be explained by a group of ordinary Humans, at least 75,000 years ago, but 170,000 is tighter, having established persistent record keeping and stuck with it. Ochre on palm fronds, knotted tendon strings, rigorously disciplined oral transmission with the Paleolithic equivalent of checksums. Basically, a stone-age Ward Christensen with a Flintstones-style X-modem Protocol. That, plus a few lucky guesses derived from first principles." Dessert had arrived, the waitress deftly maneuvering around the gesticulating Missionary.

Siggy sat back down and took a bite of his death-by-chocolate, glancing at both of the older men, still in the dark about what was going on. Ted and Stan exchanged looks.

"Well, Ted, I guess I'll be paying for the meal…"

A TELEPHONE RINGS, but WHO'S to ANSWER? THESE FOOLISH THINGS...

Not only didn't Father Gregory have Skype, or even a smart phone, he still had trouble using a push-button phone. He had always admired Charles De Gaulle, even though he was a Frank, for not having a telephone in his office.

The ringing of the old princess phone, on the knotty pine telephone table in Father Gregory's knotty pine room saved him from a night of jimmy legs and involuntary contortions; odd for the old pastor.

"Howdy!"

The voice coming in from the slim handset would be universally recognized as someone playing "phone wrestling" – whoever goes from hold to the main call loses.

"This is Sylvester Newel, secretary to Ambassador Kolya Vasiliev. Would you mind terribly holding for his excellency? But first, what is "Howdy?"

Greg didn't know the rules of the game, but he knew there was a game of some kind going on.

"Howdy is how people around here say hello. You're speaking a very crisp English for someone who doesn't know howdy. I'm sorry, I don't know any Kolya Vasiliev."

"Father, the ambassador knows you. Or, rather, knows of you."

"He knows of me? How important could this be, it's 3:00 AM here, and I must prepare for a very important conference."

"Mr. Vasiliev will be on the line momentarily. Please hold." Game, set, and match. "Yes, alright, I'll hold. I can't recall at this hour if patience is a Christian or a Greek virtue, but yes, I'll hold on."

"Father Gregory?"

"Yes. Mr. Vasiliev? Can you tell me what this is about? As I told your secretary, it's 3:00 AM here in Montana."

"Please call me Kolya. I'm acting as Special Emissary to you and your congregation…" The line cackled, coughed, and came back with a whistle.

Greg picked the phone back up.

"… of what? Special Emissary to whom? Could you repeat that, please?"

"Father, I am the Envoy Extraordinary and Minister Plenipotentiary of the Metropolitan of Moscow and all the Russias"

"Kolya, wow, does all of that fit on a business card? And you're an envoy to me, Father Gregory? I'm a parish Priest. In what sense would I rate an envoy, extraordinary or otherwise? And if I recall correctly, we were at war; are we still at war? I know we're on opposite sides of something. Shouldn't you be envoying to my boss?"

"Father Gregory, we want you back."

"Who wants me back?"

"All of Eastern Orthodoxy wants you back where you belong."

"Wow, that's impressive, have I become famous or something?"

"My mission, from His Holiness, is to propose that you bring the Antioch Church to return from the Latin Rite. You will not need to be just a parish priest anymore. The position is an improvement in your station, to say the least."

"And I get what? I'm a Priest, I really don't need that much, I don't eat a lot, I can always find a place to curl up for a nap. Aren't you poaching? I know the Pope – yes, the one in Rome – got nailed for poaching married Anglican Priests. Isn't there supposed to be an agreement about that? Really? And how would this be received in Istanbul, at St. George's? Envoy Vasiliev, Kolya. Is that short for Nicholas?"

"No, Father. I was christened Kolya. It's a tradition in my family; we'll all wind up being called by diminutives anyway, why not just start there?"

"All right. So let me get this straight. You want me to move my parish from Latin to Orthodox, and that makes me a Patriarch? What if my congregation doesn't want to go? We like things short and sweet, my congregation is working class, I don't think any of them could sit still for a six-hour wedding."

"The position comes with a palace, of course."

"A palace? What would I do with a Palace? What would I put in it, I don't really own much of anything. But really, Kolya, what's going on here? We're happy the way we are."

"You may have noticed, perhaps driving around Asia Minor, that Antioch is in Asia and Istanbul is in Europe? His Holiness would like you to change the name of your parish to the Antioch Orthodox Church of St. Peter. Keep our liturgy the way it is. The Antioch Church becomes the superior Christian denomination recognized by the Sublime Porte, over the Greek Orthodox. You get a palace and a Chevy Suburban."

"Kolya, your excellency, as I said, it is now 3:30 in the morning here. I have my notes of the call, let me look at them in the morning and I'll call you back. Yes. Certainly. About 5:00 PM your time. Goodbye."

Bzzzzt. Wrong answer. Equivocation just makes Nicky work the reel harder. Especially when it's a tie-breaker like this one. If you ever get a call from Nicky, or an email, or he shows up while you're jogging, say yes or say no, but never say maybe. It just encourages him.

Fortunately, as wrong as Father Gregory was in not just slamming the phone down, Nick was even more wrong in working the reel. The next morning, Greg got a call from Ossman Bonomo of the Turkish Capital, the Sublime Porte. What had once housed a seraglio from which the choicest concubines east of the Bosporus could be abducted, now housed a bureaucracy combining the worst elements of the original Byzantine system and the freneticism of the West Wing. To say that any output from the Porte was as unstable as Francium - 223 would be an understatement. But fortunately, by this time, Greg was catching on.

"Mr. Bonomo. Good afternoon to you. What can I do for you?" The phone did its convulsion and seizure bit again. Greg saw that you can't unscrew the mouthpiece of a princess phone...

"I'm sorry, I didn't quite catch that. Were you saying something about a security detail? Mine? I don't have a security detail."

"We know that, Father. I am from Sulime Porte security; my job will be to set up your detail. As a patriarch, you will need one, If only to maintain parity with the pope. Haven't you had some issues at your church?"

"Oh, yes, Mr. Bonomo. There were a few break-ins. Our alms box is a pretty soft target, you might say. By design. Anyone who needs to steal from a church for food, or even for liquor or opium, shouldn't also have to contend with losing a finger in the process. There's now a camera, of course, there seem to be cameras everywhere. A few times we recognized the poor soul and dropped by to help the family, the groundskeeper today is one, by the grace of God, we recognized. But no, we never saw the need for a security detail. True, a Patriarch or a Metropolitan should have a little help. But I'm just a Priest."

"You are also entitled to a helicopter?"

"A helicopter? Where would it land in Antioch? A congregant bequeathed to me in his will a Volkswagen Carmen Ghia, in my opinion a much better car than its cousin, the Porsche. At least the steering is better. And the sisters have two vans for transporting whoever needs transporting."

DingDingDingDingDing! We have a winner. Nicky worked the reel a bit too hard and it fouled, and now Greg is off the hook. One more phone call and Nick could get back to real work.

"Mr. Newel? Good afternoon to you, would you please connect me to Ambassador Vasiliev"

"Would you mind holding a moment, Father?"

"Actually, I would. Please tell His Excellency. I will not be accepting his generous offer."

The secretary did a great job of pretending to maintain his poise.

"Might I pass along a reason for your decision, father?"

"Why not? Let's just say I'm not a right fit for episcopal garb, and leave it at that, shall we?"

TнE BIC ОAY ARRIVES

Everyone started to arrive, check in, set up in the field. An ordinary, every-day sort of field, plenty of sunflowers, of course, the occasional gopher hole, 4x4 tire ruts. Who would believe, seeing this field-cum-parking lot, that it would be the base for the next incremental healing of the world?

The souvenir-laden truck made it after unloading—Nan arranged for a local to haul out a load of bottled Genuine Pure 100% Glacier Water—The Eldorado, the Gremlin, every type of vehicle that might be driven by someone under a vow of poverty or off-kilter enough to be able to hear the goats; even the White Rabbit and Furthur were dusted off and pressed into service. Who else would accept a charter to carry goats cross-country? Taich didn't have Missionaries, per se, but one day he was munching leaves outside of a carnival side-show, and the bearded lady heard him.

"This was the 21ˢᵗ Century, of course, so it was a stage beard, but it was the playing of the part that made her just special enough to hear. She had told the little goat of her wish to ride her recumbent bicycle over the Rockies, and Taich was happy to facilitate her wish. They arrived on-site with her grinning ear-to-ear and him in a little side car they rigged up. The airport was the busiest it had ever been. The roofers pulled up, putting their Airstreams, Winnebagos, and caravans in a circle at the far end of the field, Irish-traveler style, which is how they portray themselves. Except that if one of these folks does your roof, you can sleep soundly under it. And for some reason, have a goat doing your lawn while the work progressed.

Then the presumptive star of the assembly arrived in a Jeep Rubicon. The Missionary Joelle Roark, resplendent in a tailored Senior Girl Scout uniform, sash festooned with badges and insignia, some, due to a recent policy change, awarded by the Boy Scouts; her mother, Professor Connie Roark; and Mary Ann, the goat Joelle was facilitating. A 12-year-old girl could be a Missionary, but couldn't be expected to facilitate a goat traveling across the continent, and Professor Roark was a bit too stable to be able to hear Mary Ann.

One day Mary Ann showed up in the Roarks' hedged and fenced back yard. Joelle heard the goat plain as unflavored yogurt, but when her mother saw the beast munching on the hedges, she yelled at Joelle to get back in the house, and started to call animal control. "But Mom, she's a talking goat!" After Mary Ann told Joelle that most people couldn't hear her, Joelle, always the problem solver, told her mother to come down to the yard and stand next to the cute little goat. "Okay, Mom, I'm going to cross the street. Just tell the goat something that you're sure you've never told me. When you're done, hold up the rake and wave it, and I'll come back." Never one to stifle creativity, and having heard somewhere not to rain on a child's imaginary friend parade, she assented. How much damage could a little goat do? Joelle looked a little flustered when she got within range of the goat. "Sorry, Mom. Episiotomy isn't part of my vocabulary list. And I'm sure I have absolutely no idea what a husband's knot could possibly be. Sorry I gave you such a hard time being born."

Joelle was the originator of the Tweeniad, with the inspiration of Mary Ann. Students 11 to 14 years old assembled and were randomly divided into teams; different sorts of people from different places needing to work together. Even the competitions were selected randomly. Each team had to participate in two team sports, such as basketball and rugby. Each member had to participate in "brain" games, such as chess, go, and stud poker. The entire team had to put up a play, musical, or opera. Each individual contestant had to publicly perform an expository speech, a poem, or a soliloquy, or mount a painting or sculpture in the Tweeniad Gallery. And everyone had to participate in the Freelay Race: instead of passing a baton, runners relayed construction material to the other side of the track where the final runner would place it in hopes of building a free-standing structure, then go back to the beginning of the relay chain.

The winning team was the one to get all of its runners on top of the tallest structure. It was a blast, a ball, and a goof and ratings were through the roof. Every kid had friends, relatives, schoolmates and neighbors. Plus, there seemed to be an extraordinary fascination on the part of grown-ups with the doings of co-ed groups of kids with pimples and braces. Now in its third year and getting ready for a global meet, Tweeniad revenues provided scholarships for hundreds of participants, and thousands of children learned to be able to depend on people who were "other."

The highest scoring participants were invited to national assemblies and even, last year, the United Nations, to address "the future" which would be inhabited by these young people. Nobody that age wanted to fight anymore; you never knew who you were going to be teamed up with. Tugboat and Jubilee made a noble attempt at barking and howling the theme from Chariots of Fire as the crowd applauded and hoof-stamped thunderous approval at the largest and most successful Mission in years. Someone who had possibly had a bit too much to drink at the cocktail hour started passing the word that Joelle had been a child actress and co-star of a Disney picture; the crowd re-erupted with the Gilligan's Island theme song: '…The movie star, the professor and Mary Ann…"

Murmurs are like waves, they can just wash over a sea of people. It was a Google car towing an Airstream pulling up. Bronwyn and Fiona got out, along with Jim, the programmer, and Karen, the fabricator. Then Bo kicked the tail-gate ramp down, and escorted Daffid down. The tech he was wearing would have made Rube Goldberg stuff look like Hammacher Schlemmer knick-knacks. But he was walking. And his mother was crying. Was that a uniform he was wearing under the digital readouts? Bronwyn's story had spread out over the goatnet, and everyone stopped and applauded. Applauded Bo and Jim, applauded Daffid and his mom. Fiona started getting a little twitchy and Bo went over to nuzzle her. Nuzzling was a medium for large and complex messages, and Fiona and Bo understood each other, but she couldn't hear him, although Daffid could. Looked like the next generation of non-traditional family.

A party is nothing without at least one grand entrance. First we saw the vertical rows of red and green blinking aviation lights; were there planes flying straight up? Then, what were they? Helicopters? No, kites? Then the bottoms cleared the horizon. Each—what?—helikite had a gondola under it. Some of us had binoculars to see the proceedings from the back of the field; they were now trained on those whatever they were. And in the lead gondola, there was Bert the goat. His left forepaw was tied to a rope, and he pulled it down, setting off the loudest klaxon anyone present had heard, and then they landed. Goats and facilitators scrambled to run cables from the still-spinning helikites to the outdoor lighting, which would be needed soon. And, of course, it fell to JoBeth to cancel the power connection from the lodge.

It was Bert's moment to shine, to move beyond Nerd-in-Chief. *"Ladies, gentlemen, goats, noble canine guardians, anything in between. FIAT LUX!"*

Thunderous applause and a chorus of bleats greeted the spectacle of a bunch of—whatever they were—cargo and passenger carrying, power generating, steerable kites—providing that amount of power. Everyone worked out the implications. The dogs realized something good was happening and joined in with their howls. To the extent that Poodles and Cavalier King Charles Spaniels could howl. Tugboat and Jubilee, being Rat Terriers and therefore 10% hound, tried to shape the cacophony.

There was light. There was action. There were no cameras, as was the protocol. Old friends met, a grand entrance was made, and it was time for my cameo. I always make an appearance to introduce the Convocation; otherwise these people would wind up in an infinite loop introducing each other. Dan, my sweet Toozik, gave me a nod and I blew him a kiss. Showtime!

The Meeting Will Come to Order

Dan took the stage, gave the microphone its obligatory three taps, and in return received the monitor's mandatory feedback loop. Papers were squared up, glasses de-fogged, the speaker's watch taken off and laid flat on the podium. The sizing up of the crowd. The smile, followed by the look of seriousness. After the throat clearing, that would be it.

"In the name of Koen, first of the woke goats. In the name of the God served by Phineas, by Hayk, by Celsus, and now by us. In the name of those we comfort, in the name of those who protect us, of those who call the people to their Missions, literally in the name of everything that is holy, to feed the hungry, to clothe the naked, to raise up those who are bowed down, to care for the sick, to comfort the mourning. I hereby declare this, the North American Continental Great Assembly, open for business.

"The same two pieces of advice get passed around for people not all that thrilled with public speaking. Open with a joke, and imagine your audience is naked. The second part is easy, most of you already are. The first part is a little problematical. Fricka seems to have forgotten herself and started munching on my jokes printout." Dan held up the remains of the chewed pages.

"All I have left are the punch lines, so here goes.

"Do you think we should tell him where the rocks are?

"And all of the money that doesn't fall back down, He can keep.

"Five dollars, Father, just like in town.

"'Sir, please, these women are marrying Christ!' The man shook the rain from his coat and said, 'That's okay, I'm from the groom's side!'"

That last one got belly laughs and ruminant bleats; everyone must have heard it before. Dan soldiered on.

"Now that I'm fully composed, and with a much-reduced chance of, well, emitting anything aside from words, I can relate once again what has been related about 2,000 times in these Great Assemblies. Not a single goat among us has volunteered for this job. What's more, in the process, each of these goats has lost a loved one; the second goat without the bad deeds on its head, which we learned the hard way is a vital part of this procedure.

"And yet. And yet, not a single goat in thousands of years has failed to accomplish the objective: healing the world, making it incrementally a nicer place, year after year, staying at least more than a few steps ahead of the 'evil that men do.' And in recent years, more and more, not just alleviating suffering, but attacking the tools of suffering, the infrastructure of suffering, the institutional condoning of suffering. Two of this year's Missions, Mister Thang and Jenny, Joelle and Mary Ann, attacking otherness, a chief ingredient of suffering."

My sweet Toozik was unused to massive acclaim. But of the assembled, each and every one was "other." The goats were now "other" than the unselected goats. The Missionaries and facilitators were "other" than the people who couldn't hear the goats. And the Priests.

The Priests were "other" for hearing the goats, and even more "other" for whatever it was that led them to vows. This convocation played a chord setting off sympathetic vibrations in every gut present. Jampa, in his saffron robes, was the first on the dais to stand and applaud. I could see (and only someone with the perceptivity of an Original could see) the infinitesimal upturn of the lips that passed for his smile. The Buddhist Priest was past and above trivializing the occidentals' concepts of a duality of "Good" and "Evil" but he didn't want to let slip how primitive he used to think the westerners were. The Lama teaching his class would screen movies from the west: *It's a Wonderful Life, Defending Your Life, Synecdoche, New York*. Clearly there was some progress going on past the Urals. Jampa sat back down and the others followed. Dan was far from finished.

"Badness has more than one root. Xenophobia, prejudice, bias, otherness; that's only one. Failure to think, or success in thinking as long as the thinking is about how to get other people's stuff, is another root. In this year's Great Assembly, you will see a Mission that quantifies the money wasted in lack of thought and then plots a route to redirect that flow of money in such a way that thinking things through is rewarded and takes root, and at the same time pares down the Resource Conflicts, the largest share of badness, and also cares for the sick and prevents disease. No, it isn't too good to be true. And neither is this Mission completed. And it is different from other Missions in ways that will have to be discussed and debated. You've already seen the external trappings, they just flew in on those helikites.

"And then there is one presentation that breaks all the rules. It drills down to the very core of the goat project; why we do what we do. Bring flak jackets, helmets, ear plugs. Cap and Siegfried Tynan are bound to initiate warfare and demolition.

"Most of you have driven over roads recently dug up to lay fiber cable? Perhaps even on this trip to Kalispell? Those patch jobs and wobbly steel plates will break some axles and cause a few rain-on-steel slips, but when it's over, you get to have a fiber optic connection. I now turn you over to the man who keeps the show running, and you all know the odds against him and us, what he faces for even being here. Our leader, the Chief Priest, Arphaxad Cohen, Esquire. Oh, wait, sorry. It seems there's one more punch line. 'Yes, he's here. It seems he was charged with transporting a mynah across stately lions for immortal porpoises.'"

Did you know a goat could groan? I didn't. Neither did I know that dogs could do a fair pass at groaning. But the groans turned into whoots, claps, and chants of 'Arph! Arph! Arph!' as soon as Dan delivered his last line.

"Fellow sentient beings, I give you... The Chief."

Unlike some of the previous Chief Priests, Arph was a trained public speaker. When Arph spoke, the people said "Let us march" against whatever it was he was railing against that day. Arph assembled the Angry Young Man/Elder Activist Statesman combination he chose for the assembly, and began.

"Those who have vowed. Those who have been chosen. Those who have just shown up, got sucked in, or otherwise turned up in a field next to a glacier. Is there any greater proof of the value of the fruits of our bizarre and mysterious labors than this year's results? It is the youngest of us who have done the best work. And two of those three projects are work **for** the young. I've reviewed the data; youth hate crimes are significantly down in areas participating in the

Tweeniad. Bullying is down directly along the road show line followed by Mister Thang and Jenny. Bully reporting is up, but more important than that, judicial remediation in bullying cases is up.

"People learn, people's lives continue un-devastated. Everyone involved in the project wants nothing more than to tip the balance to clear bad episodes, particularly the massacres of the innocent, civilians, children, prisoners of war. It is my pleasure to announce that the largest and most unwarranted of the bad acts on our primary list, the Massacre of the Latins in Constantinople, has been cleared by the Missions of Joelle and Mister Thang, and their goat partners Mary Ann and Jenny. This victory of good over bad is made even sweeter since Jenny herself rose from being a bullying victim to accept her task and to never give up. Joelle Roark. Melissa Otterthang, now Mister Thang. Mary Ann. Jenny. C'mon up, you crazy kids! Kids, get it? Joelle, Mister. I hereby present you both with the Order Gibor v'Chcham, Hero and Wise."

Arph hung a key around each of their necks. They looked very much like Phi Beta Kappa keys, but something was odd about the keys' teeth. A close look would show that they spelled out Kadosh, Holy, in Morse code.

"This and $2.75 will get you a seat on the subway in New York. Or a slice of pizza. But those who know what it is will recognize it and you. That's more people than you may think. Jenny, Mary Ann. Here are your travel documents. You're both on the way to a petting zoo. Please except these Commemorative boxes of Chex with my compliments. Enjoy your chaffhaye and enjoy being loved by children for the rest of your natural lives. In years to come, if any part of you remembers this night, remember also how proud of you we all are."

No one present thought they would see the day that the Latin Massacre would be cleared. Christians killed by Christians, 80,000 of them. Ted, Dan, Yiorgos, and the Neophyte, Arlyn De Jesus, all hugged each other with tears flowing freely. They were no longer technical enemies. The biggest black mark on Christianity, impeaching all of the concepts of Christian Fellowship and ecumenical cooperation, would, although no one knew how, by the mysterious proceedings of the goat project, be wiped out.

"Karen, Jim, Bo. Your turn. C'mon up.

"Karen. For your mechanical assemblies and ingenious designs, please accept this Bezalel Award for Artifice in the service of humanity.

Jim, this is for you. You are now officially Guru, Rabbi, and Wizard of all things electronic. I hope you manage to learn that work can be more than just a time filler between computer games. Move beyond, continue your partnership with Karen, maybe even get a job. Just show up to an interview with that piece of paper; if anyone checks it out, you'll definitely be hired, I promise. And Bo. The Priest committee has unanimously decided to put you down on the parchment for double points. Bo, you're getting close. Keep up the good work."

Chevy, along with Bert and his crew, began grazing toward the dais.

"Fellow sentient beings. We all saw them fly in on their kite thingies. That component of their Mission just completed yesterday, and so I am giving them a chance to present directly to you. You can see the lights are on, the sound system works, all powered by those spinning things in the sky. Please welcome Chevy, Bert, and four-legged friends."

Chevy tried his best to look serious; those who knew him were impressed, but those who didn't were looking for the circus wagons.

"There are no bad results in a scientific experiment. If the hypothesis remains unproved, the experiment gets torn apart, the methodology gone over, and whatever may have gone wrong is changed; a new causal chain is chosen, the hypothesis adjusted, and soon it's hi-ho time again. The data set shows that roughly 60 million people in the United States spend more money and more time than they need to getting to work. In exchange for thousands of dollars and hundreds of hours per year, these people get the satisfaction of participating in the hospitalization and death of other people by the hundreds of thousands, with an added benefit of keeping themselves overweight.

"Two hundred thousand people per year, mainly in EPA danger and warning zones, die of irritant lung disease due mainly to tailpipe emissions; others die from smokestack emissions.

"Three missionaries were involved in the setup of the experiment. One tabulated the data, one charted the money flow, and one sought alternatives. Most households with two or more people over the age of 17 have 1.8 cars. Averages of car payments or leases, gas, maintenance, parking, insurance, and tolls are about $4,000 per year. Commutes in dense areas, which make up most of the EPA zones, can be down around the 12 to 15 miles per hour range, due to heavy traffic.

"Each regularly commuting car causes about $2,000 per year in human health care costs and agricultural losses. Carbon trade vouchers were supposed to have been traded at $20, rising to the target of $60; reality has set in and most trade at

between $5 and $13 dollars. But at $60/ton, each car removed from the road would deserve a credit of $350 per year.

"The solution is obvious. Invite people to find an alternative for one car in a multi-car household, or a part-time alternative for single-car households. Register the participants' current costs and routes. Register the alternative commute plans. Audit individual compliance. Get the European and International Carbon Exchanges to come up with some experimental funding to prime the pump. Get coastal cities to put an impost on real estate taxes to help stave off destruction.

"Health care payers should kick in two thirds of any reduced costs; one third to the participants and one third to provide alternative means of getting to work. Insurance companies should allow the typically $300 a year 'gym membership bonus' to go to people choosing to commute by human powered vehicles. National standards for electric-assist human powered vehicles so they can be sold and ridden in all 50 states. Allow any 3-wheel electric vehicle to be registered and driven as a motorcycle in all 50 states. Make sure all the participants know that the more people who participate, the more money each participant will get. This is all simple stuff.

"And this is what you get: $3,000 per year is saved on the car, about $500 per year on health care savings participant share, $300 gym credit, $300 carbon credit. That's $41,000 over 10 years, enough to at least start a kid out in college. No cap and trade, no carbon tax, no surcharges, just people saving money and lives and having fun. Oh, and you would need a social campaign signaling 'societal permission' that you won't be seen as a loser if you bike to work.

"People should jump at this, right? Wrong. The three Missionaries tried. Apparently, think tanks and centers for this or that are in favor either of 'making bad guys pay' or 'not making bad guys pay and not worrying about who gets hurt, because jobs will be saved.' We're going to try again. By the next North American Assembly, we hope to have figured out how to get people to understand arithmetic. And now I'll turn this over to Bert, with the stationary power generation side of the project. As you have seen, at least he and his team actually got something out the door!"

If empathy were a fluid, you could float the Titanic on the volume of it the Assembled had for Chevy. Everyone involved in the goat project is sensitive—goats, Priests, Missionaries, facilitators, dogs. And, of course, Originals. Sometimes we forget that most people are just not quite that sensitive. As for myself, I used to blame that on mindless TV, now I blame it on Facebook. Dolly, the fit and finish engineer on Bert's crew, made sure Bert's official engineer's pocket protector was properly clipped to his fur, and pushed him to dais steps.

"*Power does **not**, in fact, corrupt. Withholding power corrupts. Power lights things. Power saves lives with air conditioning, refrigeration, medical equipment. I usually like to let my slide rule do my talking for me, so I will keep this brief. Chevy tasked me with the component of the project dealing with reducing smokestack emissions. There is a plethora of methods for doing that. Doubling down on fusion. Thorium reactors. Even the Bill and Melinda Gates non-weaponizable reactor. Even conventional solar panels and ground-based spinners.*

"*Those last two seem to be glacial in progress relative to available land, and plagued with problems in actually getting the juice to users. And although we've demonstrated that goats can fly kites, even big ones, nuclear operations are still out of the question for ungulates. But high-altitude wind can deliver power in concentrations making it economical to run a line to even the most desolate of places. The best ground-level wind sites have average wind speeds of 15 MPH. The stratosphere has minimum wind speeds of about 75 MPH anywhere. That's 125 times the power available at ground level.*

"*Factor in the cold, allowing for thinner wires (and justifying the use of silver wiring) and take away the energy required for lift, and we're bleating about hundreds of megawatts per site, powered by **kites**. You heard Chevy say that although it will reduce carbon, this is not a climate change project, and here's why. Every single climatologist, every blessed one of the Nobel Prize winners who sign climate change petitions, every last one of them, and probably all of our two-legged friends who attended high school know it in a deep and distant memory.*

"*If you have a reservoir of hot, a reservoir of cold, and a wall between them, and you punch a hole in the wall and put a spinny thing in the hole, you generate power. The hot side cools down and the cold side heats up. The climate problem is exactly that model. We have a virtually infinite cold side in good shape, the upper atmosphere and space. Because of a carbon build up, there is now a **thicker wall** between the hot and cold sides. If you don't like how hot the hot side is, all you have to do is **punch a bl*@ting hole in the wall and put a spinny thing in the hole.***

"*We see this effect every day on the weather report; that's how hurricanes and tornadoes are powered. Any climatologist who does not start with that proposition before making a climate statement dishonors the entire scientific enterprise. Any journalist who does not begin a climate article with that proposition should go back to journalism school or cover the obituaries or the social register or something. Have the kites hoist solar tower siphons, and, if we needed to, we could actually cool the planet. People of whatever type, two or four legs, herbivore or carnivore, I thank you for your time. I'm going back to my slide rule.*"

After the head-scratching and brow-furrowing stopped, Chevy and Bert received the next wild ovation, breaking the previous record. Steve Fletcher, the native shaman on the council, was smiling. Everyone called him Two Dogs; someone told me it was the punchline of an old Indian joke. He didn't seem to mind. "May I address the chair?"

Arph looked like he could use a little break from public speaking. "Shoot."

"Father President, I may have a conflict of interest with Chevy and Bert. Although the wind and sun are free to all, these projects will need a lot of empty land. And the only thing we Natives have plenty of is empty land. If I support points for the project, it might look like I was trying to enrich my Tribe."

Arph looked at Jampa for guidance. Jampa smiled and did his job.

"Steve. Would you be trying to enrich your tribe?"

"No. I like the concept and I hope it works."

"The value of a window is in the part that isn't there. The empty part. Value is being created for your empty part, the land." As usual, Jampa, my competitor and my better at this, apparently, refrained from making a formal judgment. Arph took the stand again.

"Steve, vote as you will, without fear of ethical or procedural violation."

And the proceedings continued.

"Folks, I'd like to take the time to introduce you to some of the more creative Missions being awarded points this year. Ariel Ross, please stand up and take a bow, David, you too, let's see you wave that hoof. There we go. David's travels bore slightly more hardship than just the sins of his town. It was painful for him to hear people straining to sing. Ariel is a musicologist who could hear David; they teamed up and went to work deciding on a Mission. In 1984, Ariel heard Lyndon LaRouche run for President on a campaign of tuning A back down from 440 to 412, where it started out.

"Everyone knew that LaRourche was more than a few sandwiches short of a picnic, and the idea never went anywhere, and like every other time he ran, he didn't get a single electoral vote. Ariel started a revolving-staff opera road company, and was able to hire 20 depressed singers who could never constantly hit the highs and were unable to get steady opera work. Now they can sing, make a living, not worry about vocal cord damage, and bring entertainment to tens of thousands of people who may had never heard the *Magic Flute*, *Pagliacci*, or *Turandot*. Easing hunger is important, reducing brutality is important, caring for the sick is important. And people getting to do what they're good at while giving pleasure to others is also important. Take a bow, you two!

"Now, the other team I'm highlighting this evening deserves special recognition for completing a Mission under fire. And that's fire from all sides. Margaret Shirah, are you there? Wave to us, you brave young lady. And Billy, too, let's see some hoofing! There they are.

"Margaret's little city, for some reason, had become a hotbed of Pro-life/Pro-choice belligerency. There was a lot of yelling and screaming, uncharacteristic of the usually happy mini-metropolis. The protest violence level was starting to tick up. Margaret was reading in the park on a nice day, as she would often do, and heard Billy, who was browsing just behind the tree line. This was the first time a potential Missionary hadn't freaked out upon hearing him. He thought he was one lucky goat, and it turned out he was. Billy asked Meg what all the fuss was about; Meg did her best to explain what an abortion was and why some women might want one. Billy was trying to get his horns around it; eat and reproduce were basically what goats did. He put a thought out on the table. '*You know, when a nanny is bearing a male kid as her first birth, there's a large chance she'll die. The vet and breeder usually work out what to do.*'

"And it struck Margaret: you can work out what you should do with the help of people with your interests at heart. Didn't anyone on either side realize these women were hurting?"

"Meg took her precocious smile and serious gaze and started canvassing local merchants: Jacobson's Juvenile, a local diaper service, three day-care centers, any landlord she knew to be on the pro-life side, the very publicly conservative supermarket magnate who looked like he ate the profits, four pediatricians.

"Pretty soon Meg had fifty packets of vouchers for anything a mommy and baby would need for at least the first few years. And then she walked into the cross-fire, the oddly-named Maiden Lane Women's Clinic. Standing on neither side, but right in the middle, with her little sign reading 'I will pay your baby's expenses,' both sides simultaneously started shouting at her, 'It's not ABOUT that.' Meg couldn't make out over the din what either side's concept of THAT was.

"Then the doctor showed up in her armored Hummer accompanied by her body guards. Billy, surreptitiously browsing the devil strip just up Maiden Lane from the clinic, had the reverse-angle view of the proceedings and was the first to see the gun come out. As you all know, goats usually don't get involved in people-on-people bad interactions; that's the job of the Missionaries. But goats, as herbivores, can move pretty fast when there's danger. He hip-checked Meg out of the line of fire and charged the shooter. The shot went wild and blew the nose off the statue of Ronald Reagan in the nearby Town Square; the ricochet hit a patient who was just coming for a pregnancy check-up.

"When the dust cleared, the lady's baby was saved, the shouting died down and the shooter was caught, Meg laid out the way things were going to be. She was good at that, telling people the way things were going to be. Give us another wave, Meg! She was going to rotate clinics in turn and stand in front of each of them with her packets. She wouldn't give any out if there was any protesting, yelling, or screaming. Or shooting, of course. When she got down to her last ten packets, both sides were going to have to start funding the program. And anyone who didn't like it could kiss their flower gardens goodbye.

"And now—and I know everyone is hungry—this is what you've all apparently been waiting for. So, all creatures great and small, Siegfried Tynan and Cap."

Siggy and Cap started making their way to the front; Sig made a show of leaving his laptop behind.

"Not going to need this," he said while climbing up. Cap's been filling me on what's running through the goatnet. Everyone knows what's going on. So, I'm just going to summarize. There is a signature in the Book of Genesis, that signature is visible to, and must have been inserted by, someone who knew, so long ago, what the world's real deal was, from the cosmological to the geological to the anthropological. Big Bang, first planets, first plant life in the universe, our solar system, first vertebrates in the universe. Hominins developing symbolic communication. Hips narrowing and heads getting bigger. The loss of estrus. The switch from grass skirts to animal hide clothing. A small group leaving somewhere idyllic under harsh conditions. The start of theistic religion. The last of the Neanderthals. Megaflooding. The inventions of wine, bricks, animal-drawn long-distance transportation, the ability of grownups to drink milk. All there, all on the Genesis timeline. That signature supports the next four books, which detail that people need some fair rules to get along, play nice, and progress. Some of the rules being so successful they made from the Bronze Age to today.

"Despite the presence of talking goats, this signature does **not** mean that there is an invisible old man with a long, invisible grey beard who lives in the sky and knows if we've been naughty or nice, and maybe acts on that knowledge. It doesn't mean there's **not** an invisible old man in the sky. It just means there's a signature. And that signature gives us license to look for what's really going on.

"And finally. This project, at least for me, was pure research. Cap took a flyer that something might pop up, and it did. But as with much pure research, there is an application. People of differing religious and theological views no longer have to argue and fight with semantics, embarrassing arguments left over from the Scholastics, or obsolete Aristotelian logic. Yes, you heard right, obsolete.

"We can no longer say for sure, for the set of all things, that a particular thing is either A or Not A. There's now a piece of hard data, people can start from there and eventually find out what's really going on, including talking goats. Consider the large proportion of the goat project dedicated to resource wars and public health.

"Now consider the situation in Greater Vinegaroon County. The Cola Sisters, major fossil fuel players, and their friends fund Tim Postpone and Peter Navey at the federal level, and people like Professor Mickey Cunnyhunt at the local level. Mickey is simultaneously the head of the Greater Vinegaroon County Air Quality Board and a consulting expert representing people with business before the board. The Professor can, with the gravitas of an expert, make statements such as 'The science of pollution control is questionable because the people of Greater Vinegaroon County will never change their energy use habits.' Peter and Tim (the only House leader ever convicted of a felony) use their support from the Cola sisters to stack the electoral deck by sketchy redistricting and especially by pandering to people who hold dear to particular religious viewpoints.

"This is despite the fact that the work they do for their employers, the Cola sisters, is to **not** control air pollution which **does** sicken and kill residents of Greater Vinegaroon County. Now, no one with a particular religious or theological view, beloved or just familiar, needs to sacrifice life or health because of it. The signature can be walked back as far as it can go and people can have the maximum amount of information available about what's really going on.

"Gentle, dedicated, hard-working friends, you've earned this year's reception. I had a little taste earlier, I highly recommend the country tofu and the seitan duck. After you've had enough to drink, then you can start thinking about what this signature and its implications mean for your particular paradigm. See you when I get into my dancing shoes!"

The exterior wall of the lodge ballroom opened up onto the field, allowing the people, dogs, and goats to mix. Facilitators volunteered to take turns passing around snacks and drinks. Missionary work builds up a pretty hot head of steam, and most of it was going to be blown off tonight. And maybe some other things would be as well.

BEfORE the (I)AST

Most of the assembly was enjoying playing or watching a mean game of horn ball on the grass, dancing inside the ballroom, or engaging in maximally inebriated philosophical discussions. The advantage of having those discussions at a Great Assembly is that the person on the stool next to you is likely to know what you are talking about. But the QA team, sober as Bill W., set off to arrange its mandatory Assembly meeting. Mister Thang, as the being present least likely to be said 'no' to, was pressed into service to round up those with business before the Mast. The goats got a kick out of that, ever since it was named they all thought it stood for masticate. First stop was my suite. Mister had thought, being who he was, that he had pretty much seen everything. Upon finding me at the back of the suite, he realized that I had finally figured out how get something going with my object of desire, the Armenian Priest, physically possible for me and technically without breaking any of his vows.

"Good on yer both. But it's time to face the music, you two."

Next was Siggy, who had formally filed a request to address the Mast. When Mister finally tracked him down, in Nan's room, he saw Sig rehearsing his remarks and Nan providing feedback, both, for some reason, bereft of clothing. Always quick on the uptake, when he found JoBeth, Mister was not at all surprised to see her with Bronwyn, blowing off a little steam before the proceedings. After all, both had filed for appearances. The Walking Diversity understood that everyone needed a little something-something after completing their particular long, strange, trips; but he couldn't resist giving them a zinger.

"Anyone see the movie *Quackser Fortune has a Cousin in the Bronx*? 'How the fook can ye have a fookin' revolution if all the fookin' revolutionaries are off havin' a fook?'"

Mister liked his role as Sergeant at Arms and kept it up, escorting the party to The Clearing in the Woods, where all such ceremonies must take place. An incongruous ash tree served as the actual mast. Someone on the crew likely had both a sense of humor and a fondness for Wagner. It looked like Fiona, Bronwyn's hopefully recovering (hopefully ex) junkie daughter had already found the spot. She was as far away from the booze as she could be without risking getting lost or winding up on the glacier. Good girl. I saw she was occupying the High Seat, cuddled up with Taich.

"Evening, folks. Fiona, you and Taich look so comfortable that I hate to tell you this, but you're in Josh's chair. He doesn't always make it to these events, but we always have the chair for him."

The goat gave me a lick and a warm welcome—Good to see you Sophia.

Fiona apologized without being defensive. Nice trick. "Sorry, I didn't know, we just thought it was a good place to not be tempted by anything. Who is Josh?"

"Good question." Josh and I have a bit of an awkward relationship. If you ignore the chronology, I'm sort of his step mother. But in the finest of Downton Abbey irony, Josh holds titular rank over me. I'm aware that this sort of thing is present as well in many human families. Just then, Fiona's question was answered.

"I'm Josh. Josh is me. Pleasure to meet you." Josh's tell showed up when he saw Taich, rubbing his left palm with his right thumb, something he started doing as a baby whenever he was puzzled by something. "Please don't get up. Really, I'm more comfortable on a bench."

Fiona looked at me and then at Josh in hopes of finding out what was going on.

"How come I can hear Taich talk when I can't hear any of the other goats? It looks like anyone who can hear one goat can hear them all."

I realized that Taich was actually talking, sound waves and everything. That was odd. The chair. It all slipped into place. I gave the little goat a wink. Father Theodosius dropped by; He had every right to be there, but I didn't know what business he had before The Mast. Don't fear fear, I told myself. Then Arphraxad, our Presiding Priest, made it to the clearing, accompanied by Father Arlyn holding a little notebook, followed by Stan and Nicky. Trailing Nicky was an apparition I thought I should recognize, and I struggled to place him.

Then I smiled at him, the late Dream Team member. Was it him with the line about the glove? No, that was the one with the personality.

"Well, Bobby. May I call you Bobby? We're a little informal around here. Was it always your ambition to be the Devil's Advocate? If it was, you made it. How did you wind up in Nick's domain? It can't be because of the family you bequeathed to the world after your demise. Do you get *Entertainment Tonight* and Facebook where you are?"

The other Armenian flashed his $1,000 an hour smile. "Of course. How could you have a Gahanna without Facebook?"

"And Nicky, of course. What lawyer could possibly be sneakier and slimier than you are?

"Sophie, you wound me." The moonlight was sparkling on Nick's carapace. "Someone who represents himself in court has a fool for a client."

Last came Bronwyn and Daffid in his cyborg get-up; there would probably be some folks without business before the Mast showing up as observers. Bronwyn walked up to Arph and handed him a dollar.

"My retainer."

Mister was itching to keep going with his ceremonial role. "Does the meeting need to be called to order? Does the clearing need to be roped off or something?"

Then Taich assumed a very human sitting posture on the High Seat, Fiona still next to him.

"As Sophia said, we're a little informal around here. A little break from bureaucracy for a bit. Stan, you're the QA officer. Whaddaya say, cuz?"

"One Missionary and three Priests have been formally tested, either by myself or in conjunction with Nicky. Siegfried Tynan has admirably past the Quality Assurance stress test, and has requested Mast to address his issue. I did the taking away, and Nicky did the offering back. Father Gregory, well, I'll pass him with a gentleman's C. This was all Nicky at my behest. The Reverend JoBeth Berger is a borderline case. This was all me. I will leave it to you to decide if she has passed or failed. Reverend Bronwyn was Nicky's off-book operation. The matter is, so to speak, in Limbo. Finally, without formally testing him, Father Theodosius has violated the rule of the goat project; interfering with and spying on a Mission. I recommend having him dropped back to Neophyte, with his position to be taken over for the duration by Father Arlyn. As for the appropriateness of a Mission focusing on discoverability, it is my recommendation that the Circle of Priests should have the final say on this via their points determination system."

Taich stroked his beard with a hoof.

"Ted, is this true? Were you trying to rig the system? This belongs to the goats, you know. We just help facilitate things. Tell me what happened."

Ted made an attempt at hiding behind bureaucracy. "Um, by the way, how should we be addressing you? Never mind. We all know who we all are. By happenstance, a girl I coached in basketball wound up as a facilitator. And she called me to tell me about it. We talked, and before I realized the breach of protocol, I invited her to give me a ring if she had any questions or needed any advice. At some point, I figured out that Cap's Missionary was working on discoverability. I thought it was important, due to the nature of the Mission, to keep tabs on it. I fully understand that I transgressed and potentially harmed the project. I accept, unconditionally, Stan's recommendation. Having to move back up from the bottom will be good for me."

"If only other courts worked the same way... Anything else, Stan?"

"Bert and Chevy. They made a grand entrance and were an even grander hit at the evening meeting. But never the less, their Mission is goat-only. The goat project is to get people to do good stuff. This may be a mutiny or a revolution."

Arph nodded once again toward Jampa. The little Priest smiled once more and got ready to do his act.

"The purpose of the goat project? Is it not to get good things done? Who decided what the purpose of the project is? Do not the goats breathe the same air? Do they not eat the fruit of the same ground, on which mercury-laden ash descends? Father Arlyn. Or should I say, Pontifex of the Augustus of the West? You were the amanuensis. What is your thought on the Chevy and Bert Show? Ha, sounds like one of your morning drive radio programs. With a built-in sponsor."

"Thank you, learned master. My notes indicate that the combined financial and engineering project was not intended to be goat-only: Chevy tried three Missionaries. Stan, did you have your fingers in their inability to get anywhere? Don't answer that, I don't think I want to know."

"Thank you as well, young Pontifex." Once again, Jampa declined to judge. "My toaster would like to be enlightened as well."

Arph took the responsibility on himself. "Bert is a go. At some point they will need Missionaries to scale the project up. Chevy will be trying again; it looks like there really is a recent change in climate; political climate, anyway. Stan, Sophie, I accept the report of the QA department. We seem to still be running, if not exactly a tight ship, one that won't just decide to sink. Moving on to the requests for Mast. JoBeth, you've found yourself on Stan's list. Stan, if this is another smoking-in-the-girls-room case like last year, I may have to request Mast myself to have you moved to accounting. Say your piece, Stan, and it better be good."

Stan shot a glance at Taich. Those assembled who were Little Rascals fans got a kick out of Taich giving Stan the Hi-Sign. Then they looked at the chair and remembered what they thought was going on.

"I didn't take anything from her. I didn't harm her in any way. Anything I did was likely to have happened by itself with no help from me. This was the lowest-force stress test I ever performed, and still, she failed." I looked around and could have sworn I saw smoke coming out of her ears, but she was just nervously sucking on her e-cig. Arph was a bit hesitant to continue pushing Stan around; Arph was presiding over the meeting, but outside of Montana, Stan had height, weight, and reach on him. He looked over to the bench.

"A little help here, Josh?" Oh, the serene look. What a crowd pleaser. Josh put it on whenever he needed to buy enough time to figure the angles. Wait for it. Yup. Here it comes, first and middle fingers raised together, and here it is, the 1600 on the SATs look. Although I think that's now a 2400; why do people keep changing stuff that works?

"Stan, my dear step brother. How fondly I remember our time together in Egypt. I remember you teaching me how to skip rocks. I once got one clear across the Nile. Granted, it was a pretty dry year, but still. Then you showed me the bordello looky-lu technique. And let me assure you about that time when you went all wiggy in the desert, I don't hold that against you one bit. I know now you were under orders. You know I would have died, right? Now quit screwing around and tell us what you did and what she did to make you think she failed."

Stan tried to preserve whatever dignity he had left, shoulders back, chest out, gut sucked in. He studiously avoided looking at Taich.

"She was researching the cohabitation period. She was finding what went out as Rabbinic Academy thinking and wound up coming back as Patristics, Epistle inclusions, this or that Creed. She was tracking Moral Influence Theory. Does anyone even talk about that anymore? By the time Manichaeism showed up, the Church was strong enough to knock it over, but in the earlier period, anything went. If her last two papers had been published, she would have had enough support to go looking for the Q document." For some reason Stan looked over at Nan. "No, not the Star Trek one. JoBeth knows where all the bodies are buried. It's likely that no Journal would have wanted to risk the controversy on projects like hers. I just made sure of that. And then she cursed her own birth."

Arph put on his presidential face. "JoBeth, did you curse your own birth?"

This isn't what the catering and organizing Priest was expecting; she was the wronged party and wanted justice; now **she** seemed to be on trial.

"This is research critical for people to find out why they think and do what it is that they think and do. The research exists and people have a right to see it. I knew that I had been wronged but couldn't figure out how or by whom. So yes, I cursed my own birth. I said it loud and clear, 'Gosh darn the day I was born.' Satisfied?"

There is only the very slightest difference between the grimace of someone trying to hold in a pee and someone stifling a laugh. But then, so to speak, the dam burst. Arph was the first to snap out of it.

"'Gosh darn the day I was born'? Stan, please. 'Gosh darn.' JoBeth passes. I'm tempted to rule that you've abused the goat project to defend an intra-Christian political position. Stan, you will remove any hindrances to her publishing anything she wants. Next case, please. Oh, wait, that's Bronwyn. I'm acting as her Redeemer in this matter. Is Yiorgos floating around in the back there, somewhere? C'mon up, my trusty right hand. And don't go easy on me."

"Yia Su, Arph. And don't worry, I won't. Pastor Bronwyn, kindly step forward and state your case."

Amazing, the looks some people have. Shakespeare not-withstanding, there IS an art to find the mind's construction in the face. At least for me. Bronwyn looked at Fiona curled up with Taich in the big chair. Then at Daffid. She looked like she was thinking that she should drop this; she had her kids back. Then her face visibly changed gears. She was pissed. And what about this soul thing? Somehow you never saw Episcopalians playing chess with Death on a beach. Another gear change, double-clutch this time. I saw her taking inventory. She was a PhD, a Priest, a member of this august body, a hearer of goats, a mother. Flight never had a chance; Bronwyn was going for the kill.

"Father Yiorgos. Your Honor. I am a member in good standing in the Goat Project Council of Priests. Two weeks ago, I was engaged in the business of this Council when I was approached on line by someone suggesting he had information about my abducted children. I am, in addition to being a member of this body, a moth..."

"OBJECTION!" Bobby was up, and frothing at the mouth. "Spending time on Facebook is engaging in Council business?"

Arph stood to meet the challenge. "Your Honor. Perhaps learned counsel has not been kept informed of the upgrades. The goats are now operating as a peer-to-peer network, what we call the goatnet; there are a few nodes around; Port 799, secure socket layer, mandatory security certificate, connects the goatnet to Facebook."

"Overruled." Yiorgos, though never a lawyer or a judge, had always wanted to say that. "You may continue, Reverend."

"I accepted the terms and conditions of a software download link provided by someone I thought was a man named Nicholas Rigel. Two days later, I got my children back. One in the ICU and one a drug addict. Considerably the worse for wear since I last saw them, but at least I had them back. The on-line contact, the call, and the accident happening in such a brief window could not be a chance occurrence. I then realized that Nicholas Rigel might be our Nick. I poured through the software agreement and there it was, in a sub clause of a paragraph. An immortal soul as a condition of using the program. I am here today requesting Mast to accuse Nick of interfering with the business of the Council during the late stages of its preparations for the Assembly, and of deceptive business practices. I call for justice."

Yiorgos nodded at Bobby. "You know, I never saw the TV show your family spawned. Whenever I heard the name, I thought the show was a Star Trek spinoff from Deep Space 9. No matter, I'm just exercising a judge's right to kibbitz from the bench. Go ahead, examine the plaintiff."

"Reverend Bronwyn. Did you express an interest in having my client find your children and return them to you?"

"Yes."

"Did you accept the terms and conditions of the download and the software?"

For some reason, Arph had the beginnings of a smile. Bronwyn answered.

"Yes."

"And do you see your children here in this clearing in the woods?"

"Yes I do."

"Take a look at your daughter, Fiona. Where is she sitting, and who is she sitting with?"

"She's in Josh's seat, next to...well...a goat, but apparently a quite supreme being."

"Now, Reverend, is it possible for any recovering drug addict to be safer than in these conditions?"

"I wouldn't know. I'm not a medical expert."

"Take another look. Is she clawing at her own flesh? Is she shaking, trembling, anything like that? Pupils dilated? Nodding off? Peddling herself to the facilitators to score?"

Arph: "Objection. There's no need to humiliate the plaintiff."

Yiorgos: "Sustained. Fiona is not on trial here."

And back to Bronwyn. "The answer to each of those questions is 'no.'"

"Now take a look at Daffid. Ten days ago, he was in an ICU. And now, was he able to walk to these proceedings?"

"Yes, by means of an exo-brace rig. He's still a parapalegic."

"Take a look at his control glove. Have you seen what he can do with it?"

"Yes, I have, it's very impressive. But again, he remains a paraplegic."

"Father Yiorgos, Your Honor, members of the Council. LOOK AT THE GLOVE. IF THE GLOVE FITS, YOU MUST ACQUIT!"

Arph got up to take his turn.

"Reverend Bronwyn. Did you wet-sign the software contract? Was there a physical piece of paper? Parchment? Was there ink? Blood? At any time did you see the words 'Sell your soul?' Did you understand that the plaintiff was offering to buy your soul?"

"No, no, no, no, no, no, and no."

"Objection, Your Honor. Courts have long held that clicking on 'yes' is acceptance of an offer."

"Overruled. Courts have for far longer held that a contract must have equity, there must be a meeting of the minds."

And now the reason for the smile. "Your honor, allow me to

introduce exhibits A and B. A is the download agreement. There is no mention of anything to do with souls in this document. B is the software agreement. This, the secondary agreement, is the one mentioning souls. Although the conditions are different, the Schnabel case establishes that a supplemental agreement cannot be imposed on a user after an initial agreement was accepted. Nick was negotiating in bad faith, there was no understanding of the transaction on one side, there was no meeting of the minds, and the secondary acceptance is moot and not binding."

Taich decided to weigh in on this. "Nicky. Why don't you come home? We miss you. What has the population down there shrunk to? I heard you were down to 342; everyone else has gone through the process and moved on. Arph, I hate to pull this from you, but really, Nicky is my problem. Nick, I censure you for, without the origination or supervision of Stan, interfering in goat project preparations, and, as per the original complaint, deceptive business practices. Yes, I know, there's no other way you can operate other than deceptively. But you've crossed a line. A soul must be knowingly and willingly transacted. The contract for Bronwyn's soul is voided. But still, Nick, come home already! Arphaxad, please continue with the docket."

Nick lost another six feathers and a tooth after his censure, but he was still standing, and standing straight. Our Nick.

"Thank you. Siggy, I think it's your turn."

And then it all broke loose, hit the fan, came a-cropper, and like a carbon fiber structural support on a vibrating machine, experienced explosive decomposition and instantaneous disintegration. The Rams' Horns were sounding. Then our goats picked it up from the net. Pancovy! Pancovy! They've besieged Pancovy! That beautiful, gentle, graceful city, home of the most artistic shoemakers in the world, was under attack.

ANCESTRAL VOICES
PROPHESYING WAR

Sodomites investing the beautiful streets of Pancovy. And what streets they were. The Art Deco of The Grand Concourse in The Bronx, the Beaux Art tile work of Jerome Avenue, the whimsy of Parkchester. Gargoyles laughed and smiled from the eaves, and more than one person had tried giving peanuts to the stone squirrels. Parks and beaches where people were welcome to sleep. The Unending Mural.

The situation started brewing about four years ago. This "Prague of the West" had been flying through some heavy economic turbulence, as had many other places at the time. The shoe industry managed to hang on by, well, a shoelace. But there was pretty much nothing left for anyone else. Andreas Stern was a recently graduated architect who found himself without the possibility of employment, so he set up a stall in the public market to sell artistically designed put-it-together-yourself doll houses and playhouses. He was just barely making it, but he lived in hope.

What happened next can only be deduced through the fog of the rumor mill. Either some official's daughter was incensed when she sat on her doll house and it collapsed, or some better-connected merchant wanted Andreas' spot in the market. Either way, his life line was suddenly pulled away. Still living in hope, he invited a friend from school, similarly unemployed, to cross the border on an informal trade mission. The next country over was resource-rich but had no domestic re-investment program.

Andreas and Raf set up shop in a hotel and had a string of meetings offering Pancovy design, engineering, machine tools, architecture, skilled labor, whatever was being underused at home but would be welcomed in the neighbor country by anyone who wanted to get some business going. Needless to say, whoever's apple cart would have gotten knocked over by that paradigm decided to organize a protest outside of the hotel. Things got out of hand, and the two men were dragged out of their rooms and beaten severely, which precipitated weeks of literally incendiary protests. That began a multi-sided conflict in the region, pitting assorted historical imperatives and dialectics, as well as religious doctrines and dogmas, against each other. Due to the similarity between what happened to Andreas and Raf and a story from the *Bible*, the neighbor country was now commonly referred to as Sodom. And now Sodom had besieged Pancovy.

Two Dogs—Steve Fletcher—was the only one with cultural experience of having to choose a "War Chief," and he was put in charge of organizing whatever forces would be assembled for whatever it was the goat project or the Assembly could do. An old Mission, a pull-yourself-up-by-your-bootstraps clothing manufacturing project, was resurrected to make "uniforms." If the Assembly inserted any forces into Pancovy, they would need to have something to put insignia on to, hopefully, avoid being executed as spies.

The Knights of Velocia, a bicycle Mission from the 1970s oil shortage days, arrived at the camp. Julia, Knight Commander of Eddie, still had her braids but now they were a bright silver rather than the famous fiery red from the original promotional posters. Even the Idaho militia crowd was allowed to join, after we made sure they understood that they were not going to be shooting anyone.

Father Ted was still a commissioned officer, a chaplain in the Irish Naval Service, such as it was. He was quickly re-ranked as Admiral of the Ocean Sea, and put in charge of any refugee rescue operations. And this was a surprise: when Mister Thang was still Melissa, she (was she a he at that point, yet?) was a First Lieutenant in the US Army, serving a tour in Iraq in 2003. Since he was the only one with any real combat command experience, he became the Squid—Supreme Commander of the Quad Species Defense and Rescue Forces. Tugboat was given a little hoodie with a bird on it and commissioned as a full Colonel and put in charge of organizing the Canine Corps.

Josh granted Steve a waiver to have Koziolek brought back from the petting zoo, a very rare action that would likely cause metaphysical ripples all up and down the line. But Pancovy was his Jerusalem, he knew everything there was to know about at. He was made Chief Intelligence Officer and given a goat blanket with a Black Madonna mission patch. He stationed himself to browse in what was left of a little park near one of the main entrances to the city, to hear what he could hear. Another surprise was Daffid. While he was still technically abducted, he went to a local school and paid for it—Dick never had a reliable source of income—by joining the ROTC. He was a Second Lieutenant in the New Hampshire National Guard, and was put in charge of the relief of anyone in Pancovy with special needs.

Jim and Karen were working with Chevy and Bo to modify the helikites, which had been put into 24/7 production, for transportation, surveillance, relief supplies and, of course, local power generation. Karen was commissioned General Officer of the Salvation Air Force. Jim headed the Signal Corps, and Bo became commander of the Quad Species Corps of Engineers. Ted used what he decided would be his prerogative to line up anyone else with any type of military training and knight them as Papal Crusader Knights of St. Francis of Assisi.

Even Nicky was drafted. Under the peculiar metaphysical rules of the Originals' existence, we could demand his conscription, and if he was operating above ground, he could not refuse. He was put in charge of scaring the enemy, should we ever meet them. I was just about fairly confident he retained enough honor to do his job. Finally, Taich admitted to the leadership that he was, in fact, the Lord of Hosts. He didn't admit to being anyone or anything else, and while he could tell his rag-tag Host what to do, he had precluded himself from doing anything else. But it was a big morale booster to know that we were, at least nominally, under the command of *Adonoy T'zva'ot*. And then, of course, there was the deciding of what to do. Cap, goat of the world, been around the block a few times, not his first rodeo, knower of all the angles, was paid a great deal of deference.

"How exactly is it that supposed to play out? Precisely how can we have a war if all of us are pledged to, you know, not kill anyone? Jampa, this your department, isn't it?"

Jampa took a tentative step out of enlightenment and into what passes for reality. "Even the Sinhalese, the people who literally invented Serendipity, eventually had to execute a full assault against the Tamils, even if the purpose was to stop the killing. It is unlikely that an opposing force could be taught active awareness and become enlightened in sufficiently short order to halt hostilities."

Cap was slightly disappointed at the fall-off in purity but thankful for the invitation to practicality. *"Jammers, that's the closest you've ever been to coming down on one side or the other of a debate. Anyone else want to chime in?"*

Bert was waving a hoof like a mad-goat.

"Baki Zaki Yousef. Notice that, like myself, his name begins with a 'B.' After the 6-day War, the Israelis fortified their side of the Suez Canal. Every single officer involved, every cabinet member, probably all of the troops, knew the military doctrine that fixed fortifications were a monument to the stupidity of Man. And also, to every Israeli man, woman and child, they all think the rules don't apply to them personally. Israeli perceptions of Egyptian military capability could be summed up with this joke: 'An Arab tank and an Israeli tank collide in the Sinai Desert. The Arab gets out and says "I surrender, I surrender." The Jew gets out and says "Whiplash! Whiplash!"' The Bar-Lev Line was going to be different. The leading edge would be a very thick, steeply inclined, very high, wall of sand. You can shoot at sand all you won't and pretty much nothing is going to happen. You could never get a tank over something like that. Yousef, a Lieutenant Engineer, obviated all of that. The Egyptians started buying up high-pressure pumps, and the opening move of the 1972 Yom Kippur War was a surprise attack from the canal led by the Egyptian Engineers washing away the Bar-Lev line leading edge with high-pressure water from the Canal. The Egyptians didn't need to kill anyone to establish their position, at least in that phase of the operation. Steve, let's see what we can come up with."

And so we began. The Salvation Air Force started an air-lift relief operation with the helikites, extra gondolas added, armored, and camouflaged. The advantage of the helikite was that the higher it went, the faster it went, and the harder it was to shoot at, at least from the ground. The same was true of conventional, powered, fixed-wing aircraft, but they had to spend fuel to lift the fuel to get moving at those heights.

Food, water, and medicine were dropped by parachute; troops, human, capra and canine, were infiltrated. The sick were evacuated to hospitals outside of the conflict zone to make room for the wounded. Jim, Bo, Chevy, Karen, and Bert did a bang-up job at militarizing their project. Jim's neural net controlled a line of barrage helekites over the city. They were tied together by carbon fiber, as close to mono-filaments as Bert could get. Approaching aircraft were fouled on the lines; a cheer went up the one time they saw a Sodomite jet get its wings sliced off. Fortunately, the pilot was able to eject and regained consciousness when Jubilee was licking his wounds clean.

The dogs were divided into the black gang and the white gang; and they were pretty substantial gangs, most of the loose dogs in all six countries made their way to Pancovy. The black gang—the dogs that were actually black—snuck out at night, sabotaging, biting, or peeing or pooping on any Sodomite property. The white gang were first responders for the wounded. At least in Pancovy, it seems that dog saliva really does have, well, miraculous healing properties. An optimist or a propagandist would have termed the siege a stalemate; the reality was that Pancovy was slowly losing ground. There was a large armory in the center of town with plenty of things to use for kinetic and incendiary weaponry, and literally tons of ammunition. It would eventually run out, if the city didn't run out of shooters first. And so we come to the militarization of the goats.

Steve queried Josh, Jampa, Cap, and Taich separately. They all agreed that if someone died while trying to attack you, and you did nothing, with the possible exception of getting out of the way, you didn't kill whoever it was who died. The plan was to have Nick lead a detachment of goats into enemy territory. Nick would fly above, first as look-out, then to scare whoever showed up. Nothing would happen to him if he got shot; even though some people thought he was expendable, and the sooner the better, he was a valuable piece in the game and could do his job. As the resulting commotion got more and more chaotic, the goats would start talking, inducing whoever could hear them into surrendering or defecting. But of course, someone would have to ask the goats. And of course, the Squid, Mister Thang, was the man for that job. He posed the question to the senior goats. Then up spake brave Koziolek, the Captain of the Gate:

"Men die. Goats are born to be killed. Only the stories of their deeds live on. What better way for a goat to die than facing impossible odds, for the fodder of his homeland and the blessings of his Gods?"

The cheer that rose up almost knocked the goatnet off-line, and some of it spilled over from the port 799 interface to the public areas of Facebook. Users that day had their political arguments and clickbait posts interrupted to be treated to what looked like goats in uniforms. Another day on Facebook. But here in Pancovy, by popular acclaim, "For the Fodder of his Homeland" was emblazoned on every Salvation Air Force banner, and everyone tried just a little harder.

Nicky's goat platoons were succeeding. The tide wasn't turning yet, but now the situation really could be described as a stalemate. And he was having… I could see he was having trouble figuring out just what it was that he was having—but I could see he was having fun.

He would fly above the Sodomites and scream out "Who killed the Kennedys? After all, it was you and me!" or "Fire on the Mountain run boys, run, the devil's in the House of the Rising Sun." Our Nephew Nicky loved anything chaotic. But by the ninth mission, something must have clicked inside his sunburnt Telly Savalas skull. Trust me. I'm Sophia. Even from a thousand yards out, I can see when someone's eyes are opening. He was thinking "What in, well, Hell's name are these people doing to themselves?"

Not being an Original, he didn't have the tech manuals or update notices and, although he could do plenty of neat stuff, he never knew how or why. This is impossible for a non-Original to understand, but I'll try to map the concepts to current buzz words. When Nicky buys your soul, it creates a quantum entanglement between that precious jewel, via its Qi particles, and what would be Nick's liver, if he had a liver. The quantum ripples could be uncomfortable, and even more so as time went on, until eventually the seller would be glad to die and fulfill his or her end of the bargain. That's why Taich knew Nick's contract with Bronwyn was void, with or without the Schnable case, or wet signing, or anything else: Bronwyn wasn't entangled with anything. And it was the discomfort, even at the early stage, sub-perceptive level, that clued her in to something bad going on, not her powers of deduction. And it wasn't easy being the Common Enemy of Man.

Nicky bore the discomfort of all of the connections, but he pretended to be used to it and untroubled. Naturally, as the Father of Lies, he was best at lying to himself. With his eyes now open, that was becoming difficult. And then Nan bought the farm.

She was assigned to drive supplies around in a little deuce and a half. Cap had insisted on armoring the cab and putting auto-foam fire extinguishers all over the truck. But the wrong ends of her truck were protected: she hit a UXB from the early days of the campaign. Everyone in the city heard Cap's wail, and Sig was crying so hard that he had to be forcibly hydrated. "Everyone" included Nick. I could see something new happening to him when he was blasted by the goatnet wail. It was like he…well…felt something. And then anyone could tell he was feeling something; he was doubled over in agony, clutching his middle. Aha. No more lying to himself. Then he stood up as straight as he could and reached into what seemed to be a pocket, and looked over some papers. And then I saw he had the look of someone who had made a decision.

Nick walked in on the President of the Maximillian Republic while he was having his toe nails trimmed. Not a pleasant task for anyone undertaking it, but the esteemed leader now experienced too much agony when he tried to contort sufficiently to do the job himself. He looked up from his feet and noticed that Nick was in the room. The President glared at the trespasser. He didn't mind selling his soul to get elected, but somehow he felt cheated that he hadn't been warned about the pain. The manicurist was clearly used to seeing things in this room as weird or weirder than a shining red upright goat-looking man, and quietly left the two of them to their business. It was no concern of his, of course. Nick unfolded the first of his papers and handed it to the recently pedicured President.

"All you have to do is burn it, or tear out the signature. Before you do that, I strongly suggest you toss anything convertible to cash into a bag, put on a hoodie, walk out, and take a bus to the town you left when you first signed this. Then walk to your family's farm. The goat farm. No more pain. Goodbye, Mr. President."

Maximillian survived the abdication, but the political will to remain in the Pancovy campaign did not. Nicky achieved the same results with the Prime Minister of Ambergris and with the commander of the military government in Richland. The President of Taxavan was one of the few leaders in the region for whom Nick did not have a contract, but no matter. Taxavan was only nominally in the coalition. They sent in a team of wing-wipers to the main coalition air base to run flight condition weather forecasting, which was the limit of their involvement.

And now it was time to face the Sodomite leader. Nick held the woman's paper longer than any of the others. She was bound to be in perpetual agony. And she had erred in accepting his, well, let's call it help, just to be polite. Like the Taxavan leader, she could easily have achieved her current position through her own devices. Nick knew she would want to negotiate just on principle, and wouldn't accept relief without thinking she was getting something thrown in. Fortunately, Nick was a great believer in insurance policies.

"Madam President. Kindly inspect this other document, if you would be so kind."

The Sodomite chief didn't reply, even when she saw her own daughter's name in the box that said "Party of the Second Part."

"It's yours to do with as you please. And I strongly suggest you gather up anything of value, put it in a steamer trunk and get yourself and your daughter out of town."

I caught up with Nick back at the goat detachment headquarters. I asked him if he thought it was cricket to forge that poor woman's daughter's signature.

"Sophie, you wound me. At least for the time being, and that might be a very short period, I am still the Father of Lies, Duke of Deceit, Prince of Perjury, Count of Calumny, you get the idea. I had a job to do, and I did it. My way."

And for the first time since Enoch was alive, Aunt and Nephew exchanged smiles.

EPILOGUE
THE BIG TABLE

The Anti-Pancovy campaign collapsed in under 72 hours. While no longer being helmed by an oligarchy, the neighbor country quickly arranged a meeting with Andreas and Raf; with the logjam gone, things started getting made and sold and people started doing whatever it was they were good at, and all while being watched by the dinner party high up, at the big white table. Three hundred and forty-two people, plus Bobby, and Nick and his, I guess, cousin, Josh. And, of course, Taich. The Big Guy seemed to enjoy being small, at least for a while. Stan was there as well. Oh, and myself. The remains of the seitan duck and country tofu were cleared away. One of the volunteer serving angels stopped at Nick's seat.

"Key Lime? Pecan? Rhubarb? Apple pie? You can have it with cheddar or with ice cream, or both if you like. Or we can make you a plate with some of each."

Pie. Nicky looked around at his former…guests…seated around the table, now guests of his Uncle. And then at his Uncle, now a goat, and Josh, and Stan, and at me. And he did something I knew he didn't have the physical equipment to do. He cried. He was home.

ACKNOWLEDGEMENTS

This book is dedicated to the one I love, my darling wife, Melody Breyer-Grell, for letting me camp onto her Masters program at Wilkes University, thereby getting me in shape to write a book.

Thanks to my parents, the late Laurel Hope Grell, MA, and Ira M. Grell, CSE, for putting me square on a path of literacy and literature. Pop read me poetry every night before I went to bed; I loved The Owl and the Pussy Cat. Mom taught me how to proofread and edit.

The Bert and Chevy material on alternative energy and transportation, and their external costs, would not have been possible without the help of the late Professor Barbara Cutney, consulting philosopher. She was able to organize consequentialism and moral hazards well enough for me to present a solid concept, as opposed to being a guy on a bar stool spouting off.

The Siegfried Tynan material on the objective discoverability of a special intervention during the composition of Genesis benefited from the kind and unflagging assistance of Professor Phyllis Van Slyck, Dr. Claire Boger, Marta Joksimović of the New York Public Library, Judy Alexander, and Karen Strauss. Extra special thanks are due to Dr. Timothy J. Finney, who made sure the research material was in the best and most acceptable academic shape. I would also thank the anonymous reviewer at the Journal of Inductive Biblical Studies, but he or she is, by necessity, nameless.

Additional thanks are due to my cheerleaders, supporters, and friends at the Stuyvesant Park dog run. I would also like to thank the Wilkes graduate creating writing program, friends equally of whiskey and the written word. I consider those trips to Pennsylvania my true literary baptism.

A second nod to my wife and a shout-out to George Hoare and some whiskey for convincing me of the way to get this project going.

Last and best, Golden Fleece Press, editors and publishers, Kate Ressman and Julia Ehrmantraut, sitting at the final table along the farthest row at the 2017 D.C. Association of Writers and Writing Programs conference. By the time we got back to New York, there was an email asking for "More Goats!" And now they've presented me with something that looks, feels, and smells like a real book.

Made in the USA
Columbia, SC
03 July 2018